"Someone just blew up a car. A car that I was riding in."

Leo scooted next to Ellen and twined his fingers with hers, hoping the connection would keep her grounded and help to avoid an emotional spiral. "Maybe forensics will take a look and discover that there was some faulty wiring or a bad connection in the car, or–"

She narrowed her eyes at him. "Leo. Stop. I'm not stupid."

"You're most definitely not." He sighed and squeezed her fingers. Distant sirens told him that help was on the way. "But it turns out you're not safe here, either. Once the police arrive and we talk to them about this, I'm taking you someplace totally isolated. It'll be only me that knows where you are–"

She frowned as the sirens grew louder. "A good man died, Leo, and I'm not going to walk away when I can help bring his killers to justice."

That was unexpected. "It's not safe."

"You've kept me safe so far."

Michelle Karl is an unabashed bibliophile and a romantic suspense author. She lives in Canada with her husband and an assortment of critters, including a codependent cat and an opinionated parrot. When she's not reading and consuming copious amounts of coffee, she writes the stories she'd like to find in her "to be read" pile. She also loves animals, world music and eating the last piece of cheesecake.

Books by Michelle Karl

Love Inspired Suspense

Mountie Brotherhood

Wilderness Pursuit
Accidental Eyewitness

Fatal Freeze
Unknown Enemy
Outside the Law
Silent Night Threat

ACCIDENTAL EYEWITNESS

MICHELLE KARL

HARLEQUIN® LOVE INSPIRED® SUSPENSE

Recycling programs
for this product may
not exist in your area.

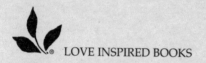

LOVE INSPIRED BOOKS

ISBN-13: 978-1-335-54395-0

Accidental Eyewitness

Copyright © 2018 by Faith Boughan

www.Harlequin.com

Printed in U.S.A.

From the end of the earth will I cry unto thee, when my heart is overwhelmed: lead me to the rock that is higher than I.
—*Psalms* 61:2

To Mom, because it's her turn.

And yes, there are Mounties in this one, too.

ONE

Ellen Biers used the edge of her T-shirt to wipe the sweat off her forehead, then stuffed the rag and bottle of lemon-scented cleanser from her other hand back into her caddy of cleaning supplies. In most of the massive luxury cottages she cleaned around northern British Columbia's Schroeder Lake in the months leading up to cottage season, the air-conditioning remained off until the residents arrived, even though the enormous picture windows sucked in heat like a sponge.

She came to the cottages to clean and maintain the interiors during the off-season, preparing them for the arrival of urban vacationers. The owners of this particular cottage weren't coming until after the May long weekend, but she'd spent extra time today making sure everything looked perfect so she wouldn't have to rush the final cleaning the day before their arrival.

She waved through a front window at Old Hogan, the landscaper who maintained the exterior of many of the same properties she cleaned, as he climbed into his weathered pickup truck. When he pulled away, she scooped up her caddy and headed back to the second floor for a final check of each room to ensure she hadn't forgotten to wipe down any surfaces or put all the knickknacks back in their places. In the master bedroom, she noticed a painting that hung askew—but as she adjusted it and stepped back to inspect the angle, a door slammed downstairs. Muffled male voices drifted upward.

Alarm constricted her insides. She'd locked the door behind her, hadn't she? The Fosters weren't due to arrive for another week. Who else had the security code to the house? With silent steps, she peeked out the doorway and saw four men milling around the base of the stairs, red bandannas tied around their mouths and black ball caps on their heads. They wore nondescript black T-shirts and jeans. As one of the men turned around to talk to the guy next to him, Ellen saw a handgun shoved in the waistband of his pants.

Handguns were illegal and difficult to come by on Canadian soil. Fear crept up the back of her throat as the reality of the situation sank in—she was trapped upstairs in a house during a break-in, and whoever these men were, they weren't your average break-and-enter "crime of opportunity" hooligans.

One of the men began barking orders. "You two, upstairs. Check the bedrooms while we hit the main floor. We have five minutes, starting—" he clicked something on his wrist—a timer on his watch, Ellen guessed "—now."

Two men thundered up the flight of stairs to the upper floor. Ellen gasped and flattened herself against the wall. If the men came to the master bedroom first, she'd be discovered immediately. Calling for help wouldn't work—she'd left her purse and cell phone downstairs, which she hoped none of the men had noticed. And the closest landline phone was in the office next door.

She briefly considered resorting to prayer, but why would God care to help her out? He hadn't been there for either of her parents when they needed Him, and as a result, she and her older brother, Jamie, had only had each other to rely on for the past fifteen years.

She held her breath and inched along the wall. Only when the men stomped off in the other direction did she dive back into the room.

Under the bed? No, surely that would be the first place they'd look. The attached bathroom? No, someone was bound to pull back the shower curtain. She glanced at the mirrored closet. What other choice did she have? The master bedroom was too high to jump out the window—best-case scenario, she'd break her leg, and the potential consequences only worsened from there. She rushed over to the closet and slid one of the mirrored doors open, cringing at the rough noise as it slid on its track. She didn't have time to wait and see if the noise had caught anyone's attention, however. She slipped into the closet, relieved when she saw that it was full of boxes, bags and piles of extra blankets and towels.

She pushed aside several boxes in the corner and dropped down, then pulled the boxes back around her as tightly as possible and draped a pile of blankets over her head. She hoped that when the thieves inevitably opened the closet searching for valuables, they'd mistake her for a messy pile of linens.

She didn't have time to slide the closet door closed the rest of the way behind her. Footsteps pounded down the hall and into the room.

"I'm telling you, I heard something," said one of the men. His voice was low and scratchy. Like it'd been damaged by years of heavy smoking.

"Don't know how you heard anything over the racket you made in the other room," growled another. This man had a slight lisp, like he was speaking around a missing tooth. "Hey, what's this we have here?"

Ellen held her breath at the sound of her cleaning supplies being slid out of their plastic caddy.

"I thought you said nobody was home."

"Nobody *is* home. We ain't seen nobody."

"Folks like this don't just leave window cleaner and stuff lying around." The man began walking around the room. Ellen's heartbeat pounded in her ears, each thud so hard she was surprised they couldn't hear it, too. Through the filmy blanket that covered her head, she made out the man's profile as he stopped in front of the closet. He looked from one side of the room to the other. Then he trained his gaze directly on the open closet door.

A scream rose in Ellen's throat as he stepped toward her—then froze as another voice called from downstairs.

"Ellen? Hey, Ellen? I saw your car by the road and thought I'd stop in to say hi—oh, hello… Excuse me…"

Ellen's jaw dropped, and horror washed over her from head to toe. The voice belonged to Rod Kroeker, a friend from the local business owners' association. Rod was a good person, a kind middle-aged man who went out of his way to help other small-business folks and bring them thoughtful gifts like coffee or donuts, or even just a friendly word on a bad day.

And today was turning out to be an awful day—but she had no idea how to help Rod without making things worse for both of them.

Turn around, Rod. Say you got the wrong house.

But the very first man who'd spoken downstairs piped up, and the men in the bedroom with her took off in the direction of the front door. She couldn't help it—she pulled off the blankets as the men's footsteps pounded down the stairs, then crept back to the doorway.

"Who do we have here?" said the first thief. "You're in the wrong place at the wrong time, mister."

Rod gasped and raised both hands as the thief casually withdrew his handgun and pointed it at the ceiling. "You're absolutely right," Rod said. "I'm so sorry. I'll be on my way."

"How did you know the door would be open?" the first thief growled. "Who's Ellen?"

Rod shook his head. "No one. A... One of the people who own this cottage," he lied. "I thought she might have come up for vacation early. Clearly, I was mistaken. I'll be going now."

The first thief waved his gun. "You won't be going anywhere."

"There's no need for anyone to get hurt," Rod said. Ellen swallowed hard on a lump in her throat as the thief waving the gun advanced on the older man. Rod backed toward the door, keeping distance between himself and the thief. "I promise, if you let me go peacefully, I won't say a thing."

"I don't trust him, boss," said one of the thieves who'd come upstairs.

"Now, listen." Rod kept backing up as the thieves moved toward him. "Like I said—"

But the man who'd been addressed as the boss lowered his handgun until it pointed at Rod. This time Ellen couldn't hold back her soft gasp, and the instant it left her lips, Rod's eyes flicked up to her hiding place as he stepped back—and in the moment of distraction, his foot caught the small lip of the door frame and he fell backward, pinwheeling his arms. Although Ellen couldn't see his entire body as he fell, there was no mistaking the hard *thwack* sound of a head colliding with a hard surface.

She watched and waited. Rod didn't move. Neither did the thieves. They seemed as stunned as she was, having entirely forgotten the noise she'd made, if indeed they'd heard it at all. After several moments, one of the men on the stairs shouted and ran down the steps and out the door.

"What did you do?"

"Is he dead?"

"Boss, did you shoot him?"

"We got what we came for, now let's get out of here! Leave it!"

Strings of curse words and shouting followed afterward. Ellen slid down into a crouch, a chill washing over her from head to toe, freezing her in place as the thieves scrambled to place blame on each other and decide what to do with "the body." There was more yelling, the sound of a heavy object being dragged and then silence.

She hunkered down there, quivering. What was she supposed to do now? What if she went downstairs and those men were outside? They'd suspected someone else had been in the master bedroom, so what if they were waiting her out? Had they actually killed Rod?

At that last thought, a wave of grief caught hold and she choked on her next breath—then stilled again at the sound of footsteps reentering the house. She didn't wait another second but dove back into the closet, grabbing a heavy bottle of bleach from her cleaning caddy as she did so.

They'd possibly killed Rod and stolen something from this house, and she wasn't going to be their next victim. If anyone so much as peeked into the closet, she'd be ready to defend herself. Her brother worked for the Royal Canadian Mounted Police. She needed to get to the phone and call for help, and he'd be here in no time—but if she had to fight her way out of this cottage to survive, she'd give it everything she had.

Her heart continued its incessant rhythm as footsteps once again came up the stairs.

"Hello? Anybody here?"

As if she'd be foolish enough to fall for that. She gripped the bleach bottle tighter and lowered her stance until she squatted behind the closet door. A creak down the hall told her that the man was checking each room in sequence. She took a deep breath in an effort to calm her shaking limbs. She tried to shove away the memory of Rod falling backward and the sound of a head meeting concrete. Dizziness rushed up to meet her as footsteps entered the room.

"Hello?" The man drew closer. His shadow passed in front of the closet. "I'm not going to hurt you—" Fingers curled around the closet door.

Here goes nothing.

The door slid open. With a scream of determination, Ellen launched herself at the intruder, swinging the bleach bottle toward his head.

The man shouted in alarm and stumbled backward, but he was too fast for her—he caught her raised arm in one hand, squeezing her wrist and twisting until the bottle tumbled to the floor. With her other hand, she slammed a fist into his gut, but he caught that arm, too, and spun her around until he held her pinned, arms behind her back. He swept his leg and she was forced onto one knee.

The tears finally threatened to spill as she gritted her teeth and prepared to keep fighting until her dying breath—when the intruder suddenly released her.

"Hang on… Ellen?" the man said.

She spun around, ready to throw another

punch—and found herself face-to-face with her brother's childhood best friend. "Leo Thrace? What are you doing here?"

He knew his mouth was hanging open, but he couldn't seem to close it. He hadn't seen Ellen in years—and the past few times he *had* seen her had been in passing, when he'd returned to Fort St. Jacob to visit his friend Jamie. Only a short drive from Schroeder Lake, Leo and his brothers had grown up on the same street as the Biers siblings, and he'd become childhood best friends with Ellen's brother. And while Leo had always had a crush on her, Jamie had made it quite clear early on that his sister was off-limits.

"I'd ask what are *you* doing here," he said, breathing heavily after the exertion of fending off her surprise attack, "but I suppose you have more reason to be in this area than I do. I'm here for my brother's bachelor weekend at the Schroeder Lake community hall."

She blinked at him and tilted her head, frowning. "Which one?"

"There's only one community hall, isn't there?"

"Which *brother*." But she didn't wait for a response, instead shaking her head, hands waving next to her shoulders. "No, forget it, that's not the right question. Did you see men outside? Or a man in his fifties with graying hair?"

"I didn't see anyone outside, sorry. There does appear to be blood on the front steps, however. Are you hurt?" He let his eyes scan her lithe form, but saw no evidence of injury. "I picked up a 911 call on my radio for this address. There are other police coming, but I was closest to the location so I came over to see if I could help."

Her brow creased. "I didn't call. I didn't get to a phone."

"Well, somebody made the call. The dispatcher gave this address."

Ellen frowned, then her features softened, and she turned sad eyes toward him. "Rod. Rod Kroeker. He must have called it in and then come inside to see if I needed help. He's such a kind-hearted person... He probably saw my car and maybe spotted the men with bandannas around their faces coming into the house and wanted to help until the police arrived..." Her voice hitched, and Leo's gut churned.

"And where is Rod now?"

She shook her head again. Her eyes had turned red and she pressed a hand against her mouth as she backed into the wall, leaning against it as if it was the only thing keeping her upright.

Oh, no. He responded as gently as he could. "The blood outside?"

She nodded, and when she spoke, her words were choppy. "He fell. I couldn't see past his waist once he fell, but it sounded like he'd been hurt and the men who broke into the house acted like he'd died—"

"Hold on. I think we'd better start from the beginning." He reached for her hand and pulled her next to him. She sank onto the end of the bed and he crouched in front of her. "Men broke into the house? How did they get inside?"

"Four, I think. Wearing black ball caps and red bandannas to obscure their faces. They were looking for something but they didn't say what—and a few of them had handguns." She glanced at him pointedly and he waited for her to continue. "I didn't hear the door getting smashed in, so either they had the code for the house or I forgot to lock the door behind me. The company that monitors the security system should be able to give the police a record of when the code was entered."

"And you didn't recognize any of these men?"

She pressed her thumb and forefinger into

the corners of her eyes. "No. I saw part of one of their faces, but it was blurred by the blanket I was hiding under. Plus, the bandanna covered from the top of the nose down. I might be able to recognize their voices, though. They were fairly distinct. Shouldn't we go looking for Rod?"

Leo ran a hand through his hair. "If there are men with handguns around, we're safest inside. And if Rod is injured, we won't do him any favors by courting danger, too. Police and an ambulance should arrive at any moment."

"But what if he's still alive and hurt?" Her voice cracked on the words, and she buried her face in her hands. "Sorry. I can't believe this. How did—" A thump sounded from outside. Ellen grabbed at his shirtsleeve.

"I'll go check it out. From inside, don't worry. I'm not armed right now, so I'm not about to dive into danger."

Ellen stared at him, wide-eyed. "But, Leo—you might not have to go outside to be in danger. Please tell me you didn't leave the door open."

TWO

He *had* left the door open. He pressed one finger to his lips to indicate they should both be quiet, then crept into the hallway. Through the bannister, he spied the open front door, but he didn't see anyone else inside. The crackle of tires against pavement brought a surge of hope. He descended the stairs, watching for movement in the house before checking the driveway through the window. An RCMP patrol car and an ambulance had pulled up, and the emergency teams were pouring out.

"You can come down now, Ellen," he called. He did a double take as she appeared at the top of the stairs and had to swallow a sudden cough of surprise. When had she become so…beautiful? The girl he'd had a forbidden crush on had been cute, with her wild red hair and freckled button nose making him sigh with frustration and adoration as a teenager. Now, her hair was still wild and bright, her nose still freckled and button-like, but she'd grown into those features and wore them with confidence. He felt a sharp jab when she focused her pale blue eyes on him from a distance. Rosebud lips turned down in a nervous frown as she began to descend the steps.

Maybe it was a good thing Jamie had long since marked his sister off-limits. Besides, what woman wanted to spend her life with a man who never had time for her in the first place? Between his RCMP position in Fort Mason, the junior high soccer team he coached half the year and his parents' fading health, his free time was scarce. He didn't even remember the last time he'd taken a day to himself to sit and read or watch a movie. There was always something else that needed doing.

His brothers had practically dragged him down here to Schroeder Lake for Sam's bachelor party, and Leo still didn't feel great about leaving the Fort Mason detachment in the hands of other people. No matter how qualified they were.

"It's emergency services," he said, turning away from her. "Let's give them your statement and then they can start searching the grounds for any signs of the intruders. Okay?"

She nodded and followed him outside as a familiar RCMP officer came running up the steps. Jamie looked from Ellen to Leo and back again. "Well, this is a surprise. Are you both all right? What's the situation here?"

Leo listened quietly while Ellen recounted the recent events to her brother. As soon as she'd finished, he and the other officer who'd driven in with him took off to do a sweep of the perimeter. They came back several minutes later, shaking their heads.

"No signs of the intruders in the immediate vicinity," Jamie said, "but I'm sure the staff sergeant will have us do a more in-depth investigation both inside and out. And I agree, that's definitely blood on those steps. Based on what you've told us, Ellen, it could mean we're looking at a homicide investigation."

Leo noticed Ellen begin to sway where she stood. Alarmed, he grabbed her arm and she steadied. "You all right?"

She shook her head no, her complexion even paler than before. "I can't do this here." She glanced at her brother. "I saw him fall, Jamie. I might have watched him die."

Leo looked sharply at Jamie, whose eyes widened with a touch of panic. "Want me to get her out of here?" Leo asked.

"Please," Jamie said, gratefulness flooding his features. "Can you take Ellen to the station in Fort St. Jacob to do the official reports? You know the drill. I'm sorry to ask this of you since this isn't your jurisdiction and you're here on vacation, but—"

"You need to stay here, I get it."

"And I don't think I'm in any shape to drive," Ellen murmured. "I'll come get the car later."

"I'll drive it home for you," Jamie offered. "I'll get it back tonight. You go with Leo."

The crackle of more tires on the unpaved driveway caught everyone's attention. A white van with a garish Rogellus logo—the BC telecom company that ran local television stations for midsize towns across the province—rushed toward them.

"And we'd better get moving," Leo growled. "Looks like I wasn't the only one listening to the police scanner for emergency calls."

"Take care of her," Jamie called after them.

"I can take care of myself," Ellen muttered once they reached Leo's car. He tried to open the door for her, but she reached ahead and did it herself, then paused. "I left my caddy inside. I need it for work."

Leo glanced back at the news van. It had parked, and a young blonde reporter was climbing down from the passenger side. "It's in the house, so it's evidence. You'll have to buy another one or claim it on your business insurance."

With a sigh, she slipped into the car, but not before the young reporter had spotted her. The woman came rushing over as Leo slid into his seat and slammed the door. He started the car and backed away, leaving the woman and her cameraman standing alone, looking more than a little upset at being denied their full story.

"You didn't want to talk to her, right?" Leo said once he'd pulled the car onto the road. "Sorry if it seems like I made that call for you. But I think it's a bad idea. You're the only witness to an incident that could turn out to be homicide, and the last thing you or the police need is for your name and face to get plastered all over the local news. You never know who's watching."

"No, it's fine. I agree, plus I want to get my story straight in the police reports before anything else. And I'm not exactly keen to have a target on my back. None of the thieves saw me, so they don't know that I might be able to recognize them—their voices, at least. I'd rather keep it that way. I might have witnessed a murder."

"Homicide, yes, but I'm right there with

you. In fact—" He glanced over at Ellen, but her head had tilted forward at a strange angle, and she looked as pale as a bleached sheet. A ragged sound came from her chest. He yanked the car onto the road's shoulder and reached for her. "Ellen! What's happening?" He pulled out his phone to dial 911 again, but she raised a shaking hand to stop him.

"There's a gas station," she said, each word breathy and forced. "Can we stop? Just for a minute. There's an attached diner with a washroom. I just need... I need to be alone for a minute."

"Of course, of course." He pulled back onto the road and gunned it, hoping his memory of the diner's location was correct. He kept an eye on her as she pressed the base of her palms against her forehead and leaned forward in her seat, nearly doubling over. Had she been hurt and not told anyone? What was going on?

They turned into the parking lot two minutes later. Several vehicles filled the gas pump stalls, and five others lined the parking spaces next to the diner. Leo instinctively scanned the area as Ellen climbed out of the car and hurried toward the door. He hustled after her, reaching the door a split second early to pull it open for her. She shuffled inside and froze, as if uncertain what to do next.

"Take whatever time you need," Leo said. "I'll keep an eye out and call the station to let them know we're on the way. I'll be waiting right here. Are you sure you don't need medical assistance?"

She nodded but didn't look him in the eye. She then took off toward the washrooms. Leo watched her until she disappeared from sight, then found a seat at the diner counter that gave him a clear view of the entire place. Several tables of patrons were enjoying their meals or cups of coffee, all absorbed in their own little worlds. One man sat in a booth with his back to the rest of the room, reading a newspaper.

Leo hoped Ellen was all right and that she'd been honest about not needing medical attention—he'd promised Jamie he'd look after his sister, and Leo meant it. Not that Ellen wasn't perfectly capable on her own, but it made sense that as her big brother and only living relative, Jamie would be overprotective of his sister.

The mumble of the television behind the diner counter caught Leo's attention, and he was surprised to recognize the young blonde reporter who'd arrived on-scene at the cottage as he and Ellen had left. The reporter was still standing in the driveway at the cottage as she spoke into a handheld mic.

"Excuse me," Leo said, waving at a server. "Can you turn the television up for a minute, please?"

The server obliged.

"…sole witness to the events here today, none other than Fort St. Jacob resident Ellen Biers. Miss Biers declined our request for an interview, however—"

Leo's stomach twisted, and a flare of fury rose in his gut. What was the reporter thinking, revealing that kind of information? She'd clearly recognized Ellen as they'd pulled out of the driveway, so was this some kind of personal vendetta because they'd driven away without speaking to her?

As the woman continued to give her report, Leo was relieved to see one of the RCMP officers at the cottage notice the reporter and head toward the camera. Surely the officer would give the news team a stern talking-to. The reporter was clearly inexperienced. Giving out Ellen's name during an active investigation was unprofessional and potentially dangerous, and possibly even worthy of a criminal charge of obstruction. The situation at the cottage was not only a theft, but a possible homicide and—if Ellen's memory had been correct—the site of illegal weapons use. The thieves couldn't just walk into a store in Canada and buy handguns. Guns were highly regulated and controlled, and it required myriad permits to own even one, let alone transport it from place to place. A gun certainly couldn't be carried out in the open.

Leo checked the time. Ellen had only been in the washroom for less than five minutes, but something wasn't sitting right. He glanced around the diner. Everyone but the man who'd been reading the newspaper remained where they'd been moments before.

And then he saw it—the plain black ball cap on the table, next to the newspaper.

Ellen leaned against the sink in the washroom, bracing herself in place with one hand on either edge. The image of Rod's foot catching on the lip of the doorway replayed over and over in her mind, the sound of his head hitting the pavement echoing repeatedly as it morphed into a much older memory. It was the same sound her mother had made as she collapsed onto the floor of their home when Ellen was eighteen years old.

Her father, an RCMP officer, had lost his life two years prior to that incident in a tragic shooting at a routine traffic stop, and her mother had never recovered. Her mother had slowly descended into darkness, and although Jamie had tried to get their mother the help she needed, well…a person couldn't be helped if they refused to accept that help.

Ellen had come home from school one day and had been surprised to find her mother in a more cheerful mood than she could remember in nearly a year. They'd hugged. Her mother had offered to make Ellen a peach-mango smoothie, having splurged on a rare treat of frozen tropical fruit. Ellen had been delighted and hopeful to find her mother acting that way.

Of course, it had all been a lie. Her mother had been chipper because she'd already decided her suffering had come to an end. Before the blender had even finished its smoothie cycle, Ellen had heard it—a thump against the counter, a body hitting the floor. Ellen had found her mother in the kitchen, seen the pills strewn about the counter and the half-empty glass of water. Emergency services arrived too late—her mother had already taken half the pills before Ellen got home, probably intending to make her daughter a snack before slipping away.

Ellen had held her mother in her arms

as the light went out of her eyes, and she'd been trying to escape the memory ever since. Sometimes it emerged when she least expected it. A sound or a smell would send her running for the safety and solitude of a washroom, closet or dark space until the memories passed. She hadn't eaten a mango or a peach since that day, the thought of both fruits leaving an ashy taste in her mouth.

If only I'd gone into the kitchen and talked to her. If only I'd asked her about her day and told her how happy it made me to see her smile again. If only I hadn't been so self-centered and sat in the living room doing nothing. I was old enough to make my own snack. I could have seen what she was doing and stopped her—

Ellen squeezed her eyes shut as her lungs tightened. She tried to force the air in and out, but her body felt like stone, unresponsive, as if her brain wanted to pour all of its energy into replaying the horrible memories over and over.

She heard a creak and loosened her grip on the sink. The diner had been a fixture on the highway to Schroeder Lake for as long as she could remember, and the plumbing was probably more fragile than she realized—much of the interior of the place hadn't changed in decades, bathroom and dining room included.

She needed to get a hold of herself. Leo was waiting for her, and she needed to give her official report at the police station before the details began to fade. She inhaled deeply and began to exhale as she opened her eyes— and screamed, throwing herself sideways as a blade flashed through the air where she'd just stood.

A burly, ski-masked man blocked the washroom exit, a knife in his left hand. With a sense of detachment, Ellen noticed the corner of a red bandanna peeking out of his plain navy blue jacket. He swung the knife toward her again. She yelled for help and ducked, dodging slash after slash in the narrow space.

"Why are you doing this?" she shouted. "Leave me alone!"

He didn't respond but grabbed for her arm instead. She kicked at his stomach as his fingers curled around her wrist, and he grunted as he stumbled backward. His large body still blocked the way to the exit, and there was no other escape. She needed to buy herself some time and keep screaming until someone heard her and came to her rescue.

With a guttural growl, the man launched himself at her again. She dove into the closest bathroom stall and locked the door, but she knew it wouldn't hold him for long. The man slammed his shoulder into the door, trying to break the lock and get inside, and the entire metal frame was flimsy enough that it rattled with each strike.

"Help! Leo!" she called over and over as she braced her own shoulder against the stall door and her feet against the wall, putting as much pressure as she could on the aging metal.

The hand holding the knife suddenly slashed at her from below, in the gap between the stall and the floor—and she took the opening it gave her. She stomped on the hand, and the man shouted in pain, dropping the knife. Ellen kicked the knife away and flung open the stall door to aim another kick at the crouching man's head.

Her foot connected, and he roared in anger. Ellen tried to run past him, but he flailed for her—and then the washroom door opened with a bang. Leo burst inside and darted toward Ellen, pulling her from the man's grasp.

"He had a knife," Ellen blurted as Leo shoved her behind him. "I kicked it away."

"Good call." Leo rushed at the man, who was scrambling for something on the floor. The instant before Leo reached him, the man sat upright and slashed at the air in front of Leo. He'd recovered the knife, but Leo was faster. He dodged the slash and kicked at the man's arm, forcing it out of the way and securing an opening to lunge in to try to take the man down. Ellen heard an exclamation of pain but couldn't tell who'd been hurt. All she knew was that they needed to get out of this situation as fast as possible, before the knife found its target.

Ellen looked around for something she could use to help Leo—a fire extinguisher or a broom, anything at all—but before she could act, the man shoved Leo aside and rushed toward the door.

He looked angry enough to kill, and he was headed straight for her.

THREE

"Ellen, move!" Leo shouted, praying she'd be able to react quickly enough to avoid being grabbed or harmed by the assailant. For a split second he feared the man's intention was to drag Ellen off with him, but the instant Ellen showed resistance by backing away and dropping her center of gravity, the man corrected course. If her attacker paused for even a fraction of a moment, Leo would have him—but the man was fast. And apparently a coward, now that he didn't have a weapon in hand to attack with.

The man burst out of the washroom and into the diner, sprinting through the eatery toward the exit. Leo followed close behind, but the assailant had a few seconds on him, and it made all the difference. Plus, the man bumped into patrons and servers as he ran, leaving extra obstacles for Leo to navigate around. Meanwhile, Leo still had no idea whether Ellen had been hurt in the moments before he'd heard her cries and rushed into the washroom to protect her.

Please let her be all right, Lord, he prayed. *I promised to keep her safe, and I'm already failing.*

The attacker headed toward a blue pickup truck sitting at one of the gas pumps, and Leo felt a rush of adrenaline in his veins. He dug deep, ready to hightail it after the truck as it pulled out of the lot—but pain suddenly tore through his kneecap, radiating outward with each step. His run turned into a fast limp as footsteps caught up with him.

"Are you all right?" Ellen gripped his shoulder and pulled herself in front of him. "Leo, did he hurt you?"

There was no time for that. He couldn't be hurt, not now. "Get in the car, hurry. We can drive after him."

Ellen's worry morphed into frustration. "Oh, no you don't. It's the police's job to go after him. The ones that actually work in this area, not you. Plus, I got the license plate number and it looks like you're in no condition to drive."

Leo returned her glare with a fierce frown. "I'm fine. The guy managed to get a solid hit on my kneecap. It'll bruise but I'll be okay. We're wasting time talking about it, though."

She placed her hand out, palm up. "The time isn't wasted. We're heading toward the police station as it is. When you ran outside, I told the servers to call the police, so they'll probably come here once they're done at the Fosters' cottage, and then head back to the station. Where *we'll* be, giving our statements. And I'm going to drive us there."

A growl rose in Leo's throat, but when he finally met her eyes, his anger melted. He wasn't upset with her. He was upset with himself for failing to keep her safe. "Fine. But there's something you need to know. That reporter at the cottage identified you on local television, which is probably how that man knew to go after you in the washroom. One of the thieves knows who you are, can recognize you on sight and knew to put your name and face together. It might have been the man who just attacked you, or someone else in his crew. I'd suspect that the group of thieves is in close contact, and they probably left one of their own near the scene of the crime to see how the RCMP would respond. Hearing that news report in the diner tipped them off to your presence during their break-in. And the guy who just got away has probably already called the others and told them about you, if they don't already know. You've become a target."

Her lips twitched downward as he placed his car keys in her outstretched hand. "He had a knife. I think he would have killed me if you hadn't heard my screaming and burst in when you did. But why kill me? Isn't that a little extreme?"

"You said yourself, you may have witnessed a homicide. And you don't know what they were searching for in the cottage. Maybe it's something incredibly valuable. Only the homeowners will be able to clarify that."

She sighed as she unlocked the car doors so they could slide back inside. There was a little more color in her cheeks than there'd been when he first pulled into the diner, but she still didn't look like she was back to 100 percent.

"Are you sure you're all right to drive?" He tried to hide his wince as he adjusted his leg placement. He needed to ice his knee before it swelled up and got any worse.

She eyed him and raised one eyebrow. "No, but I'm less sure you're any better than me right now. It's not far into Fort St. Jacob. I'll get us to the station in one piece."

They drove in silence the rest of the way

into town. Leo tried not to stare, though he had so many questions—not only about what had happened between the cottage and the diner that had made it necessary to stop, but also about her life these days. Did she enjoy her cleaning job? Why had she never left Fort St. Jacob? Was Jamie still intent on protecting every aspect of her life?

He knew it had been decades since the Bierses' father had passed away, and that they'd lost their mother only a few years later, but Jamie had never seemed willing to offer many details about it—and now was not the time to ask Ellen for the full story. She and her brother had experienced enough tragedy, and Leo definitely didn't want to pry and risk being a contributor of more emotional agony. Jamie had always implied his sister was a mite fragile. Leo had never particularly noticed this, but then again, he hadn't spent nearly as much time with Ellen as he might have liked to when they were younger.

At the RCMP station in downtown Fort St. Jacob, Ellen and Leo gave their statements and reports on both the cottage invasion and the diner incident. By the time they were done with everything, early evening had descended and Leo couldn't help noticing the dark circles under Ellen's eyes.

"You should probably turn in early and get some rest," he suggested as they headed to the front door of the station. "But I'm concerned about your safety now that your identity as a homicide witness has been leaked. Have you talked to Jamie yet about that?"

She shook her head and rubbed at her eyes with the back of her hand. "No, but I'm sure I'll be fine. We live in the same house and he'll be home tonight, so it's not as if I'll be alone."

"Yes, but if the thieves were bold enough to send someone to attack you in a public place in broad daylight, do you think they'll hesitate to break into the house of an RCMP officer? Something tells me they'd be willing to take their chances. But I'm not. I'd like to find a place for you to stay tonight that no one else knows about. Can you ask Jamie if he can suggest anywhere like that?"

As if on cue, Ellen's brother appeared in the corridor, accompanied by the detachment commander, Staff Sergeant Sherman Clyne. Jamie nodded at them both as the officers approached.

"Everything sorted out?" Jamie asked. "And did you get ice on your knee?"

"Yes, thank you. It's feeling a lot better now. Paperwork is done, reports filed, all the important things taken care of. I can take Ellen home to get some rest, but I'm wondering if that's a good idea." He held up his hands at Jamie's sudden frown. "I'm not saying you can't protect her. But we don't know where these thieves are, and her name is public. This is a small town where everyone knows where each other lives, yes?"

Jamie sighed and rubbed his eyes in a way that was so similar to his sister's, Leo might have laughed if the situation wasn't so serious. "Yeah, you're right. Not as small as Fort Mason, but small enough. What do you think, Clyne? Hotel? Or can we spare a patrol unit outside at our place?"

Clyne glanced between the three of them. "I might say motel, to be frank. I can recommend a good place."

"Does anyone care to hear what *I* want?" Ellen waved her hands. "Hello, woman who has had a really bad day here. And I don't want to stay at a motel. I'd rather sleep in my own bed."

Jamie shook his head. "It's not safe."

"I can take care of myself," Ellen retorted. "I'm a grown woman." She seemed to realize they'd fallen into a sibling fight in the middle of a police station, and her cheeks turned pink. Leo bit the inside of his cheek to keep from smiling.

"Tell you what," Leo said, an idea suddenly springing to mind. "I might know someplace you can stay, and it will be as comfortable as home but as safe and anonymous as a motel. And if the detachment can't spare an officer, I'll hang around and keep watch overnight. Does that sound fair?"

Jamie shrugged. "As long as you can promise me she'll be safe."

Leo pulled out his phone and fired off a quick message to his younger brother Sam's fiancée, Kara. "I wouldn't offer if I didn't believe that."

Ellen scowled at her brother as Leo gestured toward the front door. She followed after him, but there was no mistaking the hesitation in her steps. When they reached his car again, she paused with her hand on the door. "Leo, I appreciate everything you've done for me so far, but back there…you know I'm not sixteen anymore, right? I'm an adult and I don't need to be micromanaged. I know my brother can get overprotective at times, but I'm trying to help him see reason. Please don't fall in line with his way of treating me with kid gloves, like I'm a glass vase that will shatter at the slightest pressure."

His shoulders tensed at her admonishment. "I'm sorry if it seemed that way, Ellen. I don't mean to side with him over you. And for what it's worth, I've never thought you needed micromanaging at any age. Trust me, I noticed his overprotective nature a long time ago. So, if you're not all right with my idea, we'll decide on something else, okay? Your safety is my primary concern."

She offered a worried smile in response. "Thank you. And I appreciate that. So if I can't go home and I can't go to a hotel…is there anywhere I *can* go where they won't find me?"

Ellen tried to calm herself with deep breaths as Leo drove them across town, but her entire body was a jumble of nerves. It didn't help that she didn't really know the Parks, the people Leo had told her they'd be staying with. The Parks were the parents of Leo's brother Sam's fiancée, Kara. Leo was bringing her to spend the night at the home of virtual strangers—though he seemed to think it was a great idea, since that meant most folks wouldn't draw a connection. When they arrived at the Parks', they were welcomed with open arms, and Ellen smiled as she noticed a pair of Korean and Canadian flags hanging prominently in their front entrance.

"It's so good to meet you, Ellen," said Mrs. Park. "I didn't know your parents well, but we certainly crossed paths now and again all those years ago. Your brother is in the paper often for his police work, yes? So wonderful you've both made successful careers for yourself. Your parents would be so proud." Mrs. Park patted Ellen on the arm, and the sincerity of her words warmed Ellen's heart. "You'll of course sleep in Kara's room tonight. Leo, you're welcome to the guest room in the basement."

"Thank you so much for your hospitality, Mrs. Park," Leo said, "but I might sleep in my car to keep watch."

Mrs. Park frowned. "Nonsense. You'll be exhausted!"

"What about the couch?" Ellen suggested. She noticed another car pulling into the driveway behind Leo's vehicle. "By the window. You'll be close to the front door in case there's an issue. But honestly, I don't think it's even necessary for you to stay here at all."

He crossed his arms over his chest. "I'm staying and that's final."

Another male voice drifted in from the driveway. "It's because he'd have to sleep at a noisy cottage with a bunch of rowdy guys otherwise." Ellen glanced over her shoulder to see a younger version of Leo, with messier hair and a lopsided smile. He was accompanied by a beautiful, dark-haired Asian woman who bore a strong resemblance to the people whose doorway she stood in.

Rather than looking happy to see his brother, however, Leo sighed and shook his head. "What are you doing here? You should be enjoying your bachelor party at the lake."

"I told him that you'd called, and he wanted to come see for himself that you were both all right," said the woman, who Ellen assumed to be Kara. "I'll make him go back afterward."

"See what I have to put up with?" Sam rolled his eyes, but Kara playfully punched his shoulder and he kissed her cheek. "But seriously, are you two all right? The Parks will take good care of you overnight."

Leo winced. "Sorry about missing the party. I'd come, but I don't feel right leaving Ellen alone. Only a few people, like her brother, will know she's here, but I still want to keep an eye on her. It's not like the local RCMP detachment has many more officers than we do in Fort Mason, so it'd be difficult for them to spare someone to keep watch outside. I'm acting as a stand-in bodyguard for the time being."

Ellen blinked, surprised to hear the official-sounding label. "Bodyguard?"

"It's a good idea," Sam agreed. "Aaron and I are a phone call away if you need help."

"We'll do something together later to make up for it," Leo promised. "Before the wedding. Just the three of us."

"No worries. Nature of the job." Sam waved and headed back to his vehicle while Kara stepped inside and gestured for Ellen and Leo to follow. The family drew all the window shades closed while Leo phoned Jamie to update him on their location, and in a short time, Ellen found herself tossing and turning in a restless attempt to sleep.

She couldn't help it. Memories of her mother and of Rod's last moments flashed behind her lids every time she closed her eyes. Every creak of the house and rustle of leaves outdoors made her wonder if she was next. When light finally streamed through a crack in the curtains, she rose and made her way to the living room, only to find Leo already awake and on the phone.

He ended his call and frowned at her. "Sleep well?"

"Not particularly." His features softened

and she suddenly felt strangely bashful under his gaze. There was something in his eyes, something in the way he looked at her, which made her wonder whether he was asking as a cop, or as a friend, or because... Well, no, she was definitely imagining things. As handsome as the middle Thrace brother was, with his gently tousled espresso-dark hair and chiseled superhero jawline, he'd never see her as anything other than his friend's little sister.

"Sorry to hear that. And I'm not sure my next piece of news is going to be any better. The RCMP still haven't managed to track down the guy who assaulted you in the diner, and the vehicle he escaped in had outdated, unregistered plates. But while we're back to square one on that, your brother did some research overnight. Do you recall hearing about other vacation home break-ins recently?"

Ellen chewed her lip as she thought. "I'm sure I've heard, but they've never affected the places I've cleaned. Why?"

"Because after looking at break-and-enter reports from last year around this time and earlier this month, Jamie thinks there may be a pattern at play. Yesterday's break-in was the third vacation home robbery this month."

"Third! Why didn't the police say anything about that yesterday?"

"Because the break-ins were reported by folks like you who care for the buildings in the off-season, but there's never a sign of forced entry. And the break-ins aren't noticed until the housecleaner returns, so significant time passes between the break-in and its discovery."

Ellen sank onto the edge of the couch. "You know how lengthy the driveway is at the Fosters' cottage. It's practically a street unto itself, and I left my car all the way back by the main road because it was such a nice day and I wanted to walk. But the landscaper's truck was actually in the driveway, so they must have waited until he left and then made their move." She sighed heavily and rested her elbows on her knees. "What were they after? I didn't see anything in their hands. What was reported missing at the other places?"

Leo shrugged. "That's just it. None of these wealthy cottage owners have bothered to fly up here and look around their vacation home just to identify what's missing. They've told the police that whatever's gone, their insurance will cover it and they'll get that figured out when they fly up for the season. Let's face it, the thieves have been smart about this—taking from people who can afford to replace whatever they steal, and doing it during a time when the vacation homeowners will still be able to make an insurance claim. It's what we'd call a victimless crime."

"Except for Rod." Her throat grew thick. "Or maybe it was, until Rod. And until they came after me. So they must be making a lot of money off this scheme, or at least enough not to be willing to risk identification."

"Agreed." Leo sank onto the couch next to her. "And just because it was victimless until now doesn't make it any less wrong. I was thinking, though—it's too bad the police don't know what was taken during the thefts. If they had an idea of what's been disappearing, they might be able to anticipate what location gets hit next—after all, someone knows about these houses and what's inside. Normally, that'd make you the prime suspect since you have all the codes, but the attack yesterday at the diner certainly rules that out. And the whole attacking me with a bleach bottle thing."

Ellen's stomach growled, reflecting a mixture of anxiety, hunger and a wave of returning fear that gripped her. "So the Fosters aren't coming up to identify what's missing." It wasn't a question.

"I'm afraid not." Leo's hand landed on her knee, and she glanced at him in surprise.

Warmth rushed to her cheeks, but he looked unaffected. "And I hate to be the one to tell you this, but until these criminals are caught, going back to work is inadvisable. You're going to need to lie low, maybe even take a trip out of town. I can help you organize it. These people know your name and your face, and they're not about to let your testimony take them down. Especially since they've now become suspects in a homicide investigation."

Homicide! A lump rose in her throat and she felt her mouth drop open in response, but she couldn't find the words to ask the question that would clarify his statement. She wasn't sure she even wanted to know, but Leo anticipated her train of thought and answered it for her with a single nod and three words.

"They found Rod."

The tears came fast and furious. Leo's strong arms wrapped around her torso as he pulled her into a tight embrace, and he held her until her sobs began to abate. When he drew back and wiped his thumb across her cheeks in a futile attempt to dry her tears, an idea formed in her head.

"I can tell them what's missing."

Leo's thumb paused in its path. "Sorry, what?"

"The RCMP. I cleaned the Fosters' house

yesterday. I remember everything clearly, because I was just there. I don't have memories of other houses jumbling up the details, because I didn't go anywhere else when I finished. You said the other break-ins weren't discovered until long after someone had been there, so it was hard to identify any missing items. Well, I was literally *just there*. I can tell them what's missing, I know I can. Just get me inside to look around."

Leo cupped her face between his hands, searching her features. "Ellen... I'm not sure that's such a good idea. After yesterday, your brother..."

She pulled away from him and stood. "What about Jamie? Was he speaking as an RCMP officer or as my sibling? If he's trying to tell you that he knows my mental health situation better than I know it myself, you might want to think twice about whose voice you're giving weight to. We've already had this discussion. I'm an adult and I can speak for myself, regardless of what my brother thinks."

Leo's throat bobbed as he swallowed, but at least he was listening. She waited as he nodded, thinking. Then he pulled out his car keys and stood, too. "You're right. It's not a good idea, it's a *great* idea, and even if Jamie can't see that, I'm sure the staff sergeant will. Jamie is over at the Fosters' cottage this morning, supervising a specialist who's doing some forensic work outside, so I suggest we talk to him in person and see if we can't get access to the cottage while they're there. It'll be safer to be there at the same time as other RCMP officers, anyway."

"Thank you. Should we go right now?"

Leo held up his keys. "Yes, but the sky is overcast this morning so it's a bit chilly out. Maybe ask Kara if you can borrow a sweater or long-sleeved shirt to wear for a bit. I'll use the remote starter to get the car warmed."

Ellen raised an eyebrow at him. "The remote starter? It's not winter, Leo. That seems a tad excessive."

"Better to start the day off warm and comfortable. We may have a long day ahead of us, depending on what you spot inside the cottage and how much extra paperwork it causes." He stepped to the front door and pulled it open, looking back over his shoulder at her as he pointed the remote car starter at his vehicle. "God willing, today will be fraught with less danger than yesterday. I'll do whatever I can to keep you safe, Ellen. Regardless of how you feel about your brother's requests, that's one I'm going to uphold because it's the right thing to do."

His thumb hit the button on the remote car starter.

One second later, the car exploded in a fiery, earth-shaking boom.

FOUR

The blast rocked Leo onto his heels. As he tilted backward, he spun and grabbed for Ellen, pulling her toward him. He crashed to the floor with one hand cradled behind her head, protecting her body from projectiles or secondary explosions. The sound of crackling, overheated metal and plastic and the whoosh of flames filled the air. He counted the seconds as they passed, willing himself to wait before rushing into action. When the sound began to die down, and the explosions seemed to have stopped, he released her. She pulled back from him in a daze.

"What…what happened?" She focused past his shoulder and her mouth fell open. He twisted around to take it all in. The car was a steaming pile of wreckage, gnarled and blown wide-open. The shiny paint was streaked with scorch marks and wide, silver scratches. Flakes of debris floated through the smoky air.

Someone had just tried to kill them, *that* was what had happened. He glanced back into the house to see a shell-shocked Kara and her parents standing a few feet away. Kara had a phone in her hand.

"Call 911?" he asked.

"I just did," she said. "Are either of you hurt?"

He locked eyes with Ellen, who shook her head. "I don't think so," she said.

Leo sat upright and rolled his shoulders, bracing for pain. When none came, he breathed a sigh of relief. "I'm all right, too. I guess we're far enough away not to be hit by projectile debris."

"I have so many questions," Ellen said, her voice beginning to shake. "No one is supposed to know we're here. We only told your brother and Jamie, and while I'm sure my brother is annoyed with me on occasion, he wouldn't try to kill me."

Leo grimaced. "Sam didn't do it, and the only other people who know where we are, as far as I'm aware, are the people whose house we're in right now." He glanced over as Mrs. Park rushed over with glasses of water. "And blowing up a car risks harming their own house, so it definitely wasn't them."

Ellen took the water and drank it down in two gulps. "Thank you," she told the older woman. Then she sighed and leaned against the wall. "I admit, I'd had my doubts about whether I was really being targeted or not. When I woke up this morning, I thought maybe the knife attack in the washroom had been a coincidence, or a spontaneous reaction from the guy due to heightened tensions over what happened at the Fosters' place. But... someone just blew up a car. A car that I was riding in yesterday."

Leo scooted next to her and twined his fingers with her left hand, hoping the connection would keep her grounded and help to avoid an emotional spiral. "I was in it, too. While it's unlikely, it's possible that I'm the target instead. Or maybe forensics will take a look and discover that there was some faulty wiring or a bad connection in the car or—"

She narrowed her eyes at him. "Leo. Stop. I'm not stupid."

"You're most definitely not." He sighed and squeezed her fingers. Distant sirens told him that help was on the way. "But it turns out you're not safe here, either. Once the police arrive and we talk to them about this, I'm taking you someplace totally isolated. It'll be only me who knows where you are—"

"Yeah, I'm not okay with that."

"Ellen—"

She frowned as the sirens grew louder. "There's still an ongoing investigation that I can help with. A good man died, Leo, and I'm not going to walk away when I can help bring his killers to justice."

That was unexpected. "It's not safe."

"You've kept me safe so far." She gestured at the car. "If you hadn't started the car remotely, we wouldn't be having this conversation. So we'll just do that from now on."

"One, it's God keeping you safe, not me. He's looking out for both of us. Two, if I put you in another car, it'll be one driven by local RCMP or one the local police have examined and approved. And three…no. It's not safe to help. We can't risk it."

Her eyebrows dove toward the center of her face. "We? From where I'm sitting, I'm the one in charge of my life, not you. Are you even listening to me?" She pushed to her feet and walked to the other side of the room. "I'm telling you, I can help. If we get to the house and I can't figure anything out or don't notice anything missing, fine. Then we can talk about holing me up at a safe house. But you're an RCMP officer, Leo. You can protect me, like you said."

A lump formed in his throat as he took in the wrecked car again. "I almost didn't."

"*Almost* doesn't factor in here. Neither of us could have predicted a car bomb. But we survived, and now we keep going."

He studied her face, searching for any signs of hesitation or uncertainty. If he saw so much as a hint, he'd insist that she stay out of the investigation *and* out of sight until they figured out what was going on. As much as his emotional side might be shouting at him to hide her away in a safe place until they figured out who was trying to kill her, his practical side said that was ridiculous and unfair. He had a feeling that if he continued to insist on her staying out of things, she'd push back more and, possibly, overcompensate. He hadn't forgotten how hard she'd swung that bleach bottle yesterday. The woman turned into a fierce tigress under threat, and he didn't want to be the one her claws latched onto.

"We'll have to talk to Jamie about this first, you realize. He's taking the lead on the case, so I'm not the one you'll have to convince."

"Leave my brother to me," she said.

As the emergency vehicles pulled onto the Parks' property, Leo dragged his hand down his face. Jamie's wrath might be even worse than Ellen's—the siblings definitely had fiery tempers in common, if nothing else.

He stepped outside to greet the fire department, the first responders and the police. The two RCMP officers who'd come to the scene listened patiently before beginning their on-scene examination of the exploded vehicle. As he watched them, he pulled out his phone and dialed Jamie. He got a busy signal for several minutes until his phone lit up—Jamie was calling him back.

"Jamie, hi." He took a deep breath and prepared to launch into an explanation, but was cut short by his friend's curt laugh.

"Before you say anything," Jamie said, "I just got off the phone with Ellen. I heard the report over the radio that a unit had been dispatched to the Parks' address. She claims everyone is fine and I shouldn't worry, but I'm not sure if she's being completely honest."

Leo smiled to himself, picturing Ellen on the phone with her brother. Her eyes would have blazed and her hair would have bounced in that strangely hypnotizing way.

Someone tapped his shoulder. He glanced over to see Ellen standing next to him, hands on her hips and one eyebrow raised.

"Uh, she is," he told Jamie. "Telling the

truth, that is. But you didn't need to double-check with me, I'm not her babysitter."

Jamie sighed heavily on the other end of the line. "Just tell me she's okay and that you're still all right to look out for her today. Clearly, someone figured out where she was staying last night—though I can't imagine how—so it's best if we keep her out of the public eye a bit longer. Hunker down at the library or something."

"That's all the way back in midtown. How do you propose we get there? I'm not going to put the Parks out any more than they already have been. The explosion could have damaged their property."

"There are officers currently on the scene, correct? Have them drive you back to the station. Even better, can you two hang out at the station today instead? Order in pizza or something. We have some horses stabled out back—maybe go riding on the property if Ellen insists on going outside. There are some books in the staff room and we have great Wi-Fi."

Leo's stomach sank. He wanted to protect Ellen from danger, too, but she'd already made it clear she resented being treated like a china doll. Besides, he knew that if he were in the Fort St. Jacob RCMP's shoes, he'd want to use every available angle to solve a case, especially a potential homicide, in a town that relied on tourism to support the local economy. And a lead that depended on something as time-sensitive as a person's memory needed to be dealt with as quickly as possible.

"That sounds really relaxing, but I'm not sure that's the wisest course of action. Ellen has an idea, and while I know your first instinct will be to shut it down because she's your sister, hear me out. I'm putting you on speaker." Leo waved Ellen closer, then lowered the phone between them. "Ellen thinks she might be able to identify what, if anything, was stolen during yesterday's break-in, which might give you guys a starting point to track down these criminals."

Jamie didn't hesitate even a second. "Absolutely not."

Leo imagined that the man's stance and expression at the other end of the line was similar to the way his sister looked right now. Ellen's arms were crossed, and she'd narrowed her eyes at the phone.

"Jamie, the sooner I get inside, the more accurate my memory is going to be. And if you've been studying the case details like Leo has, you know no one has managed to identify missing items yet."

"It's not safe," Jamie growled.

"How many people have to die?" Ellen snapped back.

"Apparently one, because you—"

Leo had heard enough. "Hey! Listen. Neither of you are helping. I don't have any interest in playing referee in your sibling sparring match. Clearly, the two of you have some deeper issues to work out, but please do it on your own time. Jamie, I'm helping keep Ellen safe because it's the right thing to do and because we're friends, so I care as much about her safety as you do. And, Ellen, I'm not entirely opposed to your idea because it's potentially a case-breaking move, and because I care about justice. And as a fellow RCMP officer, I want to see justice served where I can. Even though this is technically my vacation time. Even though I should be with my brother right now, during one of the most important times of his life. So if you both don't mind, I'd appreciate it if you can set aside whatever's going on between you so we can rationally decide if Ellen going inside that house to look around is possible, practical or even safe."

Jamie sighed heavily through the phone. After a few beats of silence, he spoke. "Okay. You know what…that's actually a pretty good idea. I can't believe I didn't think of it myself, and yes, I did read all the case details over again last night after sending them to you, Leo. Do you have a safe way to get here? That's the next question."

Leo glanced at the smoking remains of his car. It was his turn to sigh. "Not exactly. And I'm on board with the idea of staying outside of public view, making sure we don't telegraph our movements to others. Maybe a van with dark-tinted windows? Or I don't suppose your team can spare someone to drive us to you."

Jamie paused. "No, we're stretched thin as it is. And a van would require you to get to a rental facility. Oh, hang on." His voice perked up. "The RCMP detachment sits at the edge of town so that there's enough room for the horses we keep out back. The back of their pasture opens onto the main trail that leads up to Schroeder Lake. If you can make your way back to the station, I'll authorize you to use the horses to reach me. No one's going to be on those paths at this time of year, and you'll be able to slip right onto them without anyone seeing—unless there's someone with binoculars sitting at the edge of police property, but the chances of that are minuscule."

Leo understood where Jamie was going

with the idea, but he still wasn't sure. "You're certain it's safer than having someone drive us there?"

"I think based on your location and the fact that someone bombed your car, yes. You've been watched. You go into the police station and leave out the back, no one is going to know."

Ellen gasped and raised her hands with her fingers spread. "I have a great idea. What if Jamie also uses a phone-finder app to track this phone while we're on the trail? That way he can see exactly the route we take and know if there's any deviation from the path. Would that work?"

"I don't see why not," Leo said, impressed with Ellen's forward thinking. "Jamie, you download the phone-finder app and I'll text you my details. Those things usually have a family-finder setting so you can trace the GPS movements exactly, right?"

"Yeah, I think so. I'll be able to see your location on my screen as you travel, as long as you have GPS enabled and there's no satellite interruption. It's cloudy today, but not too bad, so I think that will work. You'll have surveillance on you the entire time."

That settled it. Leo tucked away his phone and found Ellen standing still, staring at the ground. "Are you okay? If you're having second thoughts about going back to the Fosters', just say the word and we'll find another way to do this. Have someone walk through the place with a video camera, or..."

She shook her head in dismissal, but when she looked up, her eyes darted across the Parks' driveway to the flashing lights of the patrol cars and ambulance. "I'm fine. This is important, and if Jamie says it's safe and we'll be monitored, I trust him."

She didn't look fine, but he also wasn't going to contradict her if she felt she could do this. However, part of looking out for Ellen's safety meant considering the psychological as well as the physical. If he had to, he'd shut the operation down.

But hopefully, their findings at the Fosters' would shut down the criminals first.

Ellen swung onto the back of Boomer, one of the RCMP detachment's massive black horses, and steadied herself. She loved the highly trained beasts, and didn't get a chance to spend nearly as much time with horses as she'd have liked. She'd only met the RCMP horses a few times—they were working animals, after all—but that didn't mean they couldn't appreciate scratches and carrot snacks as much as the next horse. Their temperament was what always amazed her. For such large animals, their patience and gentleness were beyond compare. It spoke to the skill of the RCMP horse trainers as much as it did to the animals' breeding.

She sneaked a look at Leo, who'd taken the time to speak softly to Agatha, the horse he'd approached first. He scratched the mare behind the ears and kissed her snout. Only after she nuzzled into his hand did he swing up into the saddle, speaking quietly to the horse the whole time.

He noticed Ellen watching him and raised an eyebrow. "What?"

"Nothing," she said, but the word didn't feel right as soon as she'd said it. "Actually, it's not nothing. I've just never had the chance to see you interact with a horse before."

"Didn't you and Jamie have that giant dog when you were kids? It was as big as a small horse. I liked him."

Ellen rolled her eyes. "Yes, Starbuck. The Old English sheepdog was the sweetest and furriest dog in the history of dogs, but you know what I mean. Do you spend a lot of time with the horses at your detachment in Fort Mason?"

He nodded. "Aaron is more involved than

Sam and I, but I tend to spend more time in the stable than is necessary, I think. Look, horses are quiet and drama-free, compared to humans." He held up a hand at her snicker. "Compared to humans, I said! I know they have their own moodiness, but it's nice to go for a ride when I'm feeling overwhelmed. It's relaxing, and the horse I ride the most—her name is Hera—is very laid-back."

Ellen felt the next sentence press against her lips and she tried to hold it inside. This was neither the time nor the place to ask it, but curiosity compelled her to speak the words regardless. "Is she the only woman in your life right now?"

A flicker of amusement crossed his face. "My parents have this ten-year-old calico cat…"

She growled in frustration and pulled the horse out the door and outside. She led the beast toward the edge of the pasture, but the moment she reached the gate to leave the property and head onto the trails, Leo drew up alongside her.

"Are you sure you're all right to do this? Someone tried to kill you this morning. For the second time." He reached for her but she pulled away. As much as she appreciated

Leo's tendency to connect physically for reassurance, she needed to stay focused and sharp.

"I'll be fine if people stop reminding me that I should be upset," she said. "You said yourself, it's a great idea for me to go to the cottage and see if I can identify what's missing. We could be saving someone else's life here." Her throat seemed to close around her words, memories of the previous day rising to the surface. She shoved them away and blinked rapidly, trying to clear her head.

She pressed her heels into the horse's sides to surge forward and felt Leo's stare of incredulity against her back, but what she'd said was the truth. After her mother's death, people kept asking her if she was okay and acted almost angry when she'd told them she was fine. It was as if they expected her to be a blubbering mess at all times—and of course, she was one *sometimes*, but grief was a very personal and individual thing. Everyone experienced and dealt with it differently. She appreciated his concern, but the more he talked about what had already happened, the more her nerves flared.

They rode in silence down the trail toward Schroeder Lake, though Ellen didn't miss the way Leo kept pulling ever so slightly ahead of her, scanning the area for danger and keeping her at the edge of his vision. She tried to match his alertness, but it meant every rustle and every chipmunk that bolted across their path caused her to tense. Instead, she focused on the rise and fall of the horse's limbs beneath her, the softness of the clouds overhead and the way the breeze swept across the top of Leo's short dark hair.

As if sensing her eyes on him, he turned his chin toward his shoulder, about to look back. She pulled her gaze away, realizing that she'd been staring. How little she knew about this man, someone she and her brother had called a friend when they were young. Well, Leo and Jamie had been friends. She'd been the annoying tagalong, the girl who sneaked into their hangouts and conversations just to be around the cute older boy.

She'd given little thought, if any, to Leo since he'd moved away and entered RCMP training. And she would give even less thought to him after he left Fort St. Jacob and the Schroeder Lake area after his brother's wedding. So why was it taking so much self-control not to let her gaze linger over the shape of his profile, the way his shoulders squared, strong and confident, as he sat astride the horse?

Soon enough, she heard the gentle lap of

water against the lakeshore. Glimpses of its sun-kissed surface peeked through the local foliage, but rather than enjoy the view, she felt her stomach tighten in anticipation of what would be around the next bend in the trail.

"Is that it up ahead?" Leo asked once they were far enough from the main road that the lake's activity drowned out the crackle of car tires on pavement. He glanced back at her, forehead creased with concern. "If you're not up to this, just say the word. Going back inside that building after everything that happened yesterday could be challenging."

"I'm fine," she said, her words infused with the twinge of annoyance she felt at his warning. But when they emerged from the shade of the trail onto the edge of the Fosters' property, Jamie was right there, waiting for them. His arms were crossed, and a frown furrowed his brows. Anxiety flared as she met her brother's eyes. Was he having second thoughts?

She swallowed, a sudden tightness in her throat. "Dealing with what's inside the house isn't the challenge that worries me."

FIVE

Leo braced himself as Ellen's brother stalked toward them. Was his friend reconsidering the plan? They'd stayed the course on the path and hadn't seen any trouble, just as Jamie had predicted. But he looked upset—or was that guilt? Jamie kept glancing over his shoulder every few seconds, as if looking for someone. Leo noticed that another person was crouched over a patch of grass at the side of the house. He or she appeared to be scraping at the ground with a very small tool.

"Everything okay?" he called as Jamie approached.

Jamie glanced over his shoulder one last time before stopping next to the horses, hands on his hips. "I think so. Look, I can't let you in for very long. But I've done a sweep of the area and it's clear. Old Hogan has been landscaping all morning at another place just down the way, and he hasn't noticed anything unusual since he arrived."

Leo didn't miss the hesitation in Jamie's voice. Something was keeping the man from feeling fully comfortable with the plan. "I know you're the lead on this, but have you cleared our visit with your staff sergeant?"

Jamie's gaze snapped to his, the muscles around his neck and jaw growing tight. "I didn't. Ellen is a civilian, and this isn't your jurisdiction. I'm sure I could make a compelling case, but it'll take time for approval and Clyne is in a meeting this morning."

Ellen slid from the back of her horse, gripping the reins. She patted Boomer's neck as she spoke. "Wouldn't he want me in there, anyway? The sooner I get inside, the more accurate my memory is going to be. And if you've been studying the case details, you know no one has managed to identify the missing items yet."

Jamie reached across and took the horse's reins from Ellen. "Honestly, I don't think we'd even found any kind of connection between these break-ins until yesterday, when the events forced us to take a closer look. There are a lot of random break-and-enters up here, but you'd be surprised how many times it's not caused by humans but by distressed wildlife. Young deer jumping through glass windows, raccoons getting inside through the chimney, that kind of thing."

Leo ran a hand through his hair. "We don't have that many wildlife break-and-enter calls up in Fort Mason, but I can see how being close to the lake would attract more wildlife, especially during wildfire season."

"Yep. And without the ability to determine what's missing—and without any leads—we haven't had a reason to expend further energy or assign our already limited resources to it."

Leo tried not to let his relief show too overtly. "So we're good to go inside? We'll be quick. I think Ellen already has an idea of where to look."

"I do," she said, interlacing her fingers and pressing outward. One of her knuckles cracked. "I was inside while the men were walking around, so I have a pretty good idea of which rooms they went into and what route they took while in the house. I couldn't see all of them at all times, but they weren't in the building for that long. They had only so much time to traverse the place and find what they were looking for. I'm quite certain I over-heard one man set a five-minute timer once they'd entered the cottage."

"Yes, I remember reading that. And you

know they found what they wanted? That was in your statement yesterday, too, right?"

Ellen nodded. "I heard them say they'd found what they were looking for, so I assume that means exactly what it sounds like."

Jamie flicked his gaze down the driveway and back toward the house. "All right. You can go in, but I can only give *you* five minutes." He held his hand up as Ellen began to protest, but Leo wasn't surprised. The man was taking a huge personal risk by letting them inside at all. "I'm sorry, but that's the best I can manage. I'm going to talk to the staff sergeant as soon as he's out of his meeting, but I don't want to press the limits too much. Only touch what you absolutely need to, take your shoes off at the door and—"

"I've got it," Leo said. He patted his friend on the arm. "In and out, no touching. We're on the same team, remember?"

"Right." Jamie's features relaxed even further. "Of course. Sorry."

As they approached the porch, the person working in the grass looked up in alarm. Now that they were closer, Leo understood—she was a forensic examiner, likely checking out either a blood spatter or footprint. He smiled at her with a wave of acknowledgment, but she scowled, and her attention snapped to Jamie. *So that's who he was watching for.*

"Officer Biers! Who are they and why are they entering my crime scene?" She stood and marched toward Jamie, her voice rising with irritation.

"They're here as part of the investigation. Leo is Fort Mason RCMP, and—" Jamie began, and though Leo tried not to eavesdrop, he couldn't help overhearing the woman as she shouted.

"We're not in Fort Mason, Officer, this is a homicide investigation, not a chance to let your friends play Nancy Drew. There's no way the staff sergeant consented to this."

"Please, Ms. Trucco, if you'll just let me explain."

"There's no explaining an officer allowing unauthorized individuals into my crime scene—"

Leo grimaced. The forensic examiner had every right to get upset, and if she called the staff sergeant and insisted on pulling him out of his meeting…well, the dynamics of this investigation could get messy very quickly. He hurried to catch up with Ellen, who'd already reached the porch—but instead of kicking off her shoes to head inside, she stood at the edge, frozen in place.

"Ellen?" He gently touched her arm and leaned in. Her gaze was fixated on a spot by the front door. *Where her friend had fallen.* "Hey. I don't want to rush you, because this can't be easy, but we don't have a lot of time. If you're okay to do this, we need to go inside right now. But if you don't want to, or you can't, that's all right. Just say the word or walk away if talking is too much. I won't be upset and neither will anyone else."

Ellen blinked several times then inhaled through her nose, her rib cage visibly expanding with the depth of her breath. When she reached the end of her exhale, she raised her head, kicked off her shoes and proceeded into the house.

Leo's hands tightened into fists by his side, but his earlier anger at the attacks against Ellen had abated to a simmer. Rather, he felt a need to suppress the urge to reach for Ellen, to reassure her once again that he'd keep her safe—even if he hadn't done a great job of it so far. At least he'd managed to prevent a fistfight between siblings, something he'd had plenty of practice with while growing up.

He'd always been the one in the middle when Aaron and Sam fought, his brothers sometimes swinging at each other to the point of bloodied noses and black eyes. And Sam

had usually started it. What a difference a few
decades and some life experience made. Now
he couldn't remember the last time the three
Thrace brothers had fought, save for the few
times they'd raised their voices in disagree-
ment about a case. But those were professional disagreements. Nothing like what he'd
seen between Ellen and Jamie.

He followed her inside. She stood at the
front door and swept her gaze across the
room, a wide, open-concept living room
space with massive picture windows at the
front and back. To the right was the stair-
case up to the loft-like second floor, with a
balcony-style hallway that overlooked the living room and the bedrooms at the back. Leo
allowed himself a moment to marvel at how
much a vacation cottage like this must have
cost, but quickly re-centered his thoughts as
Ellen moved farther into the room.

"They stopped to talk here," she said, ges-
turing to the base of the steps. "Then two of
them went upstairs while the others stayed
downstairs and looked around. I hid when
the guys made their way up to the second
floor, so I didn't see where the downstairs
crew searched. I only heard the men up here
as they went into each room. Maybe that's
where I should start?"

Leo nodded. "Do it. But don't linger."

She hurried up the stairs and he followed behind, giving her space to work but staying near enough to be of assistance if she needed him. As she proceeded through each room, her shoulders grew increasingly tense and she shifted her weight more often. The frustration began to roll off her in waves, especially when they reached the master bedroom where she'd hidden during the break-in. She didn't even glance at her caddy of cleaning supplies, fully focused on the task at hand.

"They weren't in here long," she said. "Mostly they came in this room, almost found me in the closet and then went back down when Rod—when they were interrupted." She spun and exited the room, heading back down the stairs. "I don't think it's up here, Leo. If they found what they were looking for like they claimed, it's got to have come from—"

"And just what do you think you're doing?" A muffled yell turned clear and loud as the front door banged open. Staff Sergeant Clyne burst inside, face red with anger, his body puffed up like a fighter ready to take his turn in the ring. The forensic examiner followed him, looking triumphant, and a shamefaced

Jamie shuffled close behind, attempting to get a word in.

Leo's hopes sank as the detachment head stormed into the room, shaking his finger at them. Ms. Trucco stood at the doorway with her arms crossed.

"You have no right to be in here, Officer Thrace. This is not your detachment, and this is not your case." He turned to Jamie. "And I hope you like desk work, because letting them in here is a total lapse in judgment. They're compromising a crime scene, Biers. This was not your call to make. What did you think, that you could hide this from me? If Trucco hadn't called me, you'd have let these people destroy all our potential evidence—"

Jamie's expression darkened. "With all due respect, sir, I believe it is my call. I'm the lead on this case, and I made a judgment call. Not a lapse. Trucco is a visiting instructor for our detachment, not the person in charge, so if you'll just allow me to explain—"

"Not the person in charge? Well, now neither are you. Get out."

Leo glanced over at Ellen, expecting a crestfallen woman who was cowed and discouraged by the staff sergeant's fury. Instead, she stood by the wall closest to the base of the stairs, next to an oak hutch covered in greenery-filled planters. Her hands were behind her back, and her face remained uncharacteristically expressionless.

"Time was of the essence," Jamie pleaded. "As I was trying to explain to Ms. Trucco, I have every good reason—"

"Get them out of here." Staff Sergeant Clyne ignored his officer's pleas, turned on his heel and stomped out. "And I expect to see you back at the station as soon as the next officer arrives to relieve you. Ms. Trucco, please continue with your work. Keep me apprised of any developments."

Leo watched as the staff sergeant returned to his vehicle and climbed inside. The man didn't start the car, though—he appeared to be waiting to ensure that Jamie made good on his orders.

"Sorry," Jamie said, sweeping his hand toward the front door. "That's what I was afraid of. I didn't expect him to get so upset, though. He was in a meeting—I thought he'd appreciate me waiting to speak to him. Guess he's more worried about impressing Trucco than I realized."

Ellen side-eyed the scowling examiner, who'd returned to her work in the grass but was keeping a close eye on the trio. "Who is she? I don't remember seeing her in town."

"Laura Trucco. Visiting instructor for the skills upgrade course I told you about. It ended yesterday, and she was supposed to fly out in the evening, but then…" He shrugged and stepped aside to allow Leo and Ellen to leave the house and put their shoes back on. "She offered to help, since she's here, anyway. Has tons of qualifications. The course was excellent, too. Your brother came down early to take it, Leo."

"That he did. I didn't recall the name of the instructor, but now that you mention it, it sounds familiar." Leo clapped his friend on the shoulder. "Hopefully we'll come out of this with something useful one way or the other. And Trucco aside, Clyne's probably extra-sensitive about having a homicide in a tourist area. It's nerve-racking at the very least and can have serious negative economic consequences, so I wouldn't take it personally."

"Isn't that the truth? I'm sure he'll see reason once I've had a chance to explain. He tends to run a bit hot under the collar in general, but I know how to handle him. I guess you didn't learn anything, though?"

Leo glanced at Ellen, who shrugged.

"Maybe," she said, her voice low and quiet. "Look, I don't want to get you in any more trouble than you already are, so we'll head back to town and keep the GPS going on Leo's phone, but…you should talk to Old Hogan again before you leave." Leo followed her gaze and saw a gray-haired, stooped figure working on a flower bed several cottages away. "Here, take this. Go ask him about it." She inclined her head toward Old Hogan and pretended to bump Jamie's shoulder playfully, as if the siblings were teasing each other, but Leo didn't miss the subtle handoff of something from Ellen's palm to Jamie's pocket.

Jamie fixed his sister with a stern stare—then glanced toward the landscaper and back at her. "Ellen, I *can't*. Clyne is still sitting there in his car and Trucco keeps glaring at us. You heard my orders, I'm off the case. I have to head back to the station immediately. I can't risk a formal reprimand or a suspension. I could get pulled off duty without pay. But I'll be looking closer at the reports again. I liked Rod, too—he was a treasured member of our community, and I want to see his killers brought to justice as much as anyone."

Ellen's face fell. "Hogan is right there, though. This could help solve the case."

"I know," Jamie hissed. "But I can't risk my job based on a hunch. I'll check out my, uh, pocket and talk to him as soon as I can, but I can't do it now."

Leo knew immediately what he had to do. "I can."

Jamie looked sharply at him. "My superiors are watching, and they want you gone."

Leo nodded. "We'll be gone—we'll be, what, fifty meters away? And not on this property, so we're both following orders. And we'll be safe because, like you said, they're watching. Trucco is trying to pretend not to, but she's not doing a very good job of it. Either way, you don't have to risk your job. We ask a few time-sensitive questions under armed police supervision and then head back to the station. We have to return the horses, anyway."

Jamie sighed. "Are you sure? If you learn anything, call me immediately. The quicker we move on this case, the better, because with a homicide to contend with in addition to the break-ins…the very simple fact is that even if the thieves didn't intend for loss of life during their robbery, it happened. And if they get away with it, psychologically they're less likely to be as careful the next time, because they'll know they can cover up their wrongdoing without consequence. Solving this could literally mean life or death for the next person who crosses the thieves' path."

Ellen nudged her brother with her elbow. "I understand. Leo's RCMP, too, remember? He'll know what to say. We'll keep the GPS on Leo's phone so you can track us once we're back on the trail. We'll see you back at the station." Ellen gave her brother a quick hug and hurried off to the horses. Leo followed. Once they were mounted and out of earshot of Trucco and Clyne, Leo reined in his horse and cleared his throat.

"All right, let's hear it." He looked pointedly at Ellen's hands. "What'd you hand off that I'm talking to this guy about?"

She pressed her lips together, then let them spring open. Leo had to look away, feeling a strange spark of adrenaline as he noticed the shape of her mouth. What was that about?

"I found something in a planter at the bottom of the stairs. I'm certain it wasn't there before the men arrived, because I always start cleaning in the living room first. I clean out the dead leaves from the planters and water them." She sighed and wrinkled her nose as if smelling something unpleasant. "I found a squished cigarette butt. I don't know why the forensic examiner didn't find it first, but… we're going to talk to the man it belongs to."

* * *

Ellen took a deep breath before plunging into her explanation. "Old Hogan does landscaping on the vacation cottages. He manages the outsides while I clean the insides. Well, his full name is Keith Hogan, but everyone just calls him Old Hogan since he's been a fixture in the area for decades. He's a nice enough person, but he smokes a lot and the butt I found is his brand."

Leo eyed her with skepticism. "How could you possibly know that?"

"The smell." She tasted the memory of bitter smoke on her tongue. "He only smokes these awful, cheap cigarettes that he imports from a reserve in Ontario. Don't ask me why, he tried to tell me about it once—something about his childhood and where he grew up—but I didn't listen. I wasn't exactly interested in a story about cigarettes. But his vice may work in our favor. He's not supposed to be inside the houses. He only cleans the outside, but this is definitely his."

"You should have handed it directly to the forensic examiner if you were that sure."

She looked over her shoulder toward the Fosters' cottage. The rear porch was visible, along with Trucco's back. "I wanted to give it to Jamie on the down low, because the staff sergeant was too angry to take us seriously, the forensic examiner was too incensed to listen to anything Jamie had to say and I didn't want to hand it over while they were yelling at him. The way Trucco was behaving, I honestly worried that she might grab it out of my hand and throw it away or something. I don't have a clue why she didn't find it first, but hopefully it'll provide Jamie with enough of a lead to get back into Clyne's good graces."

Leo glanced back, too. The staff sergeant still sat in his car. He probably wanted to be sure they didn't try running back into the house as soon as he drove away. "I'm not sure I agree with your methods, but I understand your reasoning."

He followed Ellen's detour off the path to the back of the cottage where Old Hogan was working. "Didn't you say yesterday that Hogan had gotten in his truck and left the Fosters' property only minutes before the men who broke in arrived?"

"I did." Ellen thought back to the day before, trying to reconcile the timing in her mind. "He left and then they showed up. I thought they'd waited for him to leave before breaking in, but his leaving could have been a cover-up for what came next. Though I don't know that he'd have had the necessary time to take his truck far enough away that the police couldn't see it, *then* make his way back to the house."

"What if there was another driver? Hogan could have sped down the road, dropped off his truck and met up with the crew."

Ellen thought about it, but something didn't feel right. "Maybe. But the timing still seems odd…" She groaned, and her horse whinnied softly. She leaned over to scratch behind the animal's ears. Boomer seemed to appreciate it. "I don't know, Leo. I just don't know. This is the best thing we have, though, and Jamie might be able to make something of it that I can't."

"You do realize that if the cigarette was his, it makes him a suspect." Leo checked again for Clyne's patrol car. He was still there. "Then again, we've got an armed RCMP officer watching our six, so I guess there's that."

They reached the edge of the cottage property where Old Hogan was working and dismounted. The path down to the flower beds was rocky and not good for the horses, and besides, Ellen didn't want to ruin his careful landscaping. She'd known Old Hogan for nearly her entire life—he'd been landscaping in the area since her grade school days—but she didn't know much about the man. It seemed unconscionable that he could be involved in theft and homicide, but then again, she had full confidence that had been his cigarette butt in the Fosters' planter.

As they walked down toward Old Hogan, Leo squeezed her shoulder, and for some odd reason, her heart did a little hop at the same time. She shut it down by refusing to think about it, the same way she refused to think about a lot of things that bothered her. Bottling it all up was the only way to cope, the only way to avoid a descent into the madness of memory.

"Do you know what you're going to say to him?" Leo asked suddenly. She paused and he stepped in front of her, placing his hand on her hip with his back to Old Hogan. Like he didn't want the man to overhear them—or her to go bolting over and tossing out a volley of random questions. "Here's the thing. While he's not a suspect yet, he will be as soon as Jamie processes the evidence—that is, if you're right about what you found. But the fact of the matter is, the thieves are still out there. These people tried to kill you, and even though I can see you're trying not to let it bother you, it should. A car bomb isn't a matter to take lightly, and neither was the washroom attack. We need to stick close together, and I need you to continue letting me take the lead."

His voice lowered as he stepped toward her, and only then did she notice that his hand hadn't left her hip. It lingered there, the warm pressure of his fingers suddenly making her very aware of the small distance between them. "Does that sound fair?"

Her throat seemed to close again…but this time, his fingers resting against her hip were the culprit.

"Sure," she managed, though the word felt strange as it left her lips.

Was it fair that he wanted to watch over her? Of course. Was it fair that her long-abandoned childhood crush on this man had suddenly been rekindled by a few heroic gestures and the gentleness of his touch?

Not at all.

SIX

Leo winced internally as a strange, unreadable look came over Ellen. She nodded as if she understood and agreed with him—and then pulled away, hurrying down the path toward the landscaper. Leo spared a glance back in the direction of the Fosters' place. Sure enough, the staff sergeant's patrol car was still there, though Jamie's was now gone and a new car had arrived. The forensic examiner, on the other hand, was now wandering around the Fosters' backyard, and if Leo wasn't mistaken, appeared to be tossing glances in their direction a little more often than necessary.

He made a mental note to ask Aaron if she'd been so intense in the course she'd taught, too—some specialists were just like that. As long as they did good work, abrasive attitudes were allowed to slide. Nature of the business, it seemed—plus, specialized skills like forensic examination weren't exactly a dime a dozen, so often supply and demand with experts came into play on larger cases.

Leo followed Ellen down the path, noticing the immaculate design and care of this cottage's exterior grounds. Close-cropped green grass was framed by neatly trimmed hedges, and flower beds dotted the wide yard in an asymmetrical pattern. The flowers were bright and lively, evidence of a skilled hand at work in the harsher climate of northern BC.

"This is…really good." He raised an eyebrow at Ellen.

"There's a reason he gets hired by the big city folks, and you're looking right at it."

"If all his work is like this, I'm not surprised. It's exceptional." After the events of yesterday and this morning, there was a strangeness to the beauty of the property. His adrenaline kept him expecting someone to jump out at them from around the corner or for a nearby object to randomly explode, but his brain knew it wasn't rational. They were using horses for transportation—and it was nearly impossible for someone to tamper with them unnoticed.

Besides, they were dealing with thieves. Thieves didn't *want* to get noticed. They operated in the shadows, under cover of anonymity. If another attack came, it would make sense to expect it at night or during the twilight hour, when visibility was at its lowest, or—he glanced up at the sky, noting the large mass of gray clouds rolling in from the west—under any conditions that provided some level of cover.

That didn't mean he and Ellen could afford to relax their caution, however. And to their advantage, they were being watched by several fellow law enforcement professionals, even if it was out of frustration or suspicion that they might interfere with a crime scene.

From the angle they approached Hogan, they only saw the top of his head, but as they came closer, it was clear they'd interrupted the man during his lunch break. He was seated on a piece of decorative driftwood, a sandwich raised halfway to his mouth. A donut sat on a napkin next to him, and a silver thermos rested at his feet. His skin was wrinkled and leathery, evidence of long days spent out in the sun without protection.

The closer they came to him, the more the air reeked of sweet, pungent cigarette smoke.

Leo sneezed in an unintentional announcement of their arrival, startling the older man. He sneezed twice more, the cigarette smoke bothering his sinuses more than usual.

"Eh? Ellen? What on earth…?" The man lowered his sandwich and squinted at the two of them. "Welcome to my, er, office, I suppose. And who's this?"

Leo scanned the area as Ellen came forward. Nothing about this man gave off an air of danger or aggression. Rather, he seemed confused.

"Hi, Hogan," she said. "I'm going to skip the small talk and get right to the reason we're here."

Leo did a double take. Where was this side of Ellen coming from?

She took a deep breath and continued. "You might have heard about what happened at the Fosters' yesterday. After you left."

Hogan nodded and folded the wrapper back over his sandwich. "Got a visit from a couple of officers, but I already told 'em I don't know anything. Didn't see nothing after I left. Went to the store, bought some muffins, went right home."

"You live in town?" Leo asked. He noticed Ellen raise an eyebrow at him. Of course she already knew the answer to that.

Hogan frowned. "Of course I do. Who are you?"

Ellen sighed pointedly at Leo and continued, "One of your smokes was found inside the Fosters' place in a planter. As if some-one put it out, got startled and accidentally left it there. And before you ask how I know it's one of yours, give me some credit. We've worked on the same properties for years, and I know the smell of that special brand you bring in from out of province. Which I'm not even sure is legal. Is it legal, RCMP Officer Thrace?"

Hogan shifted abruptly on his seat, as if someone had jolted him with a small electric shock. He stared at Leo.

"Lots of regulations surrounding the im-port of tobacco from out of province," Leo said. "I hope you've got all your paperwork in order."

The man flinched, but Leo had an inkling it was out of surprise rather than fear. If Ellen knew that the man imported these products, so did Jamie, and undoubtedly so did the rest of the local RCMP. Either the man really did have his permits in order, or the local detach-ment looked the other way when it came to this particular situation—and either way, it really wasn't any of Leo's business.

"Never you mind about that," the man mut-tered, likely picking up on the same things Leo had. "But I never went into the Fosters' place, not once. I'm no dummy. I've been working on properties in this town and at the lake for thirty-odd years now, and I'm not about to jeopardize my business. Not when I'm on the verge of retirement, you hear?"

Leo slid his gaze across to Ellen, who regarded the older fellow with almost apologetic pity. "The cigarette butt got inside the house somehow, and Ellen here insists that you're the only one in the area who feeds his vice with this particular brand. Might I add, these things are going to kill you someday, sir."

Hogan snorted. "As if I don't know that? I'm too old to change. Too far in now, son. Can't fix an old badger like me. But I tell ya, I don't know how it got in there." The man's gaze went squirrelly, darting from place to place.

Gotcha, Leo thought, stepping closer. "You sure about that? I want you to think really carefully about what you say next, sir. A man died yesterday. A treasured community member. And so far, the only thing the police have to go on is a cigarette butt from a brand you're known to smoke. At this point, you're the prime suspect." Or at least, he would be once Jamie had the go-ahead from the staff sergeant to resume work on the case.

Hogan's eyes widened like saucers and he

dropped his hands to his lap. "You know, now that I think about it…a few days ago, a customer came to see me. I have a little office space. Biers here knows where it is. Wore a hat and sunglasses. Sat right across from me, early morning when the sun was coming up and streaming through the window, you know? I had to squint to see him through the sun's brightness. He pulled out his pack at the end of the meeting, but it was empty. Asked if he could bum a smoke. I…well, I gave him a few, because he was talking about bringing in a lot of business. A couple of new properties on the west side of the lake. Said he was a developer, looking to fix up the exterior so's he could sell or rent at a higher rate."

The man's story sounded reasonable enough. "Did the man leave his name? With a big proposition like that, he must have."

"Hah, you'd think." Hogan shook his head and raised his sandwich back to his mouth. "Took my smokes and I haven't heard from 'im since. Still might. Sometimes takes a while for folks to decide. Lots of options around here, but my work speaks for itself."

Leo ran his hand through his hair and looked over at Ellen, who responded with a small shrug. She didn't know whether to believe him, either.

"So what you're telling me is that a client came to see you, dressed like a person trying to disguise himself, proposed a whole bunch of new business, then took some items from you that are commonly known to be used by you and you alone." Hogan nodded. "And then those items were found at a crime scene a few days later."

Hogan froze, mouth hanging open. Leo recognized the moment the man understood what was going on.

"I don't suppose," Leo said, "you have a security camera set up at your office?"

The landscaper's face fell. "No, Officer. There's an alarm on my shed with all the tools, but nothing like that. Never needed it." He dropped his sandwich back into the wrapper, almost missing the edge of the checkered paper. "I'm being framed, Officer. Surely you can see that."

I can also see that you didn't start respecting authority until it seemed like you might be in trouble, Leo thought. "I recommend that you think a little harder about what might have happened that day, and I recommend even more strongly that you pay a preemptive visit to the police station and tell them exactly what you told me. But with more detail and specifics. Understand?"

Old Hogan nodded, but his chin drooped as Leo escorted Ellen back up the path toward the horses.

"I feel bad for him," Ellen said as soon as they were beyond earshot. "I don't think he had anything to do with this."

Leo began to untie the horses. "I don't, either, but the fact remains that he's connected somehow through those cigarettes. And I have a feeling he knows more than he's letting on. Like the identity of the person he gave the smokes to, perhaps. He looked awfully upset when he put the pieces together—disappointed, even. Hopefully if he does know who it is, he realizes that they took advantage of him in a big way and aren't worth protecting."

"Loyalty runs deep in small towns, though," Ellen said. They mounted the horses again and headed back to the trail. Leo couldn't resist a quick wave at both the forensic examiner and Staff Sergeant Clyne. Trucco didn't acknowledge them, but Clyne raised two fingers. The moment their horses hit the trail, they heard a car engine start and tires crackle down the driveway.

As impressed as he was that Ellen had known who the cigarette butt belonged to, Leo couldn't help but feel like they'd come full circle and were back at square one. Unless Hogan could identify the person to whom he'd given the cigarettes, they had nothing left to go on.

"Back to the precinct?" Ellen asked after several minutes. "I don't want to spend the rest of the day and possibly the night at the police station, but that's the safest course of action. Jamie told us to come back, and he's monitoring your phone's GPS, after all." She sighed, her full, red lips tilting downward.

Why do I keep noticing her lips? Leo mentally kicked himself and began to pray. *Now is not the time. Lord, please help me to stay focused. I know Ellen thinks she's fine, but she has lived through so much trauma, and I'm not sure how to help her. As a friend. Only a friend.*

Jamie would never forgive him if he even entertained a thought of anything more.

Suddenly, Ellen gasped and pulled the horse to a halt. She snapped her attention toward him, hair twisting around her face at the force of the movement. "Leo! Do you still have that list of homes that reported break-ins? Or could you convince my brother to send it to you?"

"I do have it. I was reading through all the reports last night. Why?"

She raised one of her hands skyward. "I

know you said the reports of the break-ins were inconclusive and that no one has made a connection yet, but some of these happened last season, right? So we can presume that some of the owners eventually came back to their cottages, depending on the timing of each robbery."

He nodded, not entirely certain where she was going with this.

"Some of those cottage owners had to have discovered what was missing, even if it was months and months later. And they probably wouldn't have bothered to report anything, because they'd already had their insurance payout, or it seemed like a hassle, or who knows. It could be any other reason. But I can't believe that *no one* has figured out what the thieves took. That literally makes no sense."

"Okay, but what can we do about that? If they didn't report it, how does that help us?"

Ellen smiled, suddenly beaming, and Leo felt the reins slip from between his fingers in surprise. He hadn't seen a proper smile on her since…he couldn't remember since when. He scrambled to re-grip the reins and keep himself upright on the horse as she laughed softly.

"I'll ask them. I'll phone the cottage owners and ask them up front. If they don't want to tell me, that's fine, but why wouldn't they? I'm sure they'll understand when we explain the reason for asking."

"That *is* a good idea." He thought for a moment about the logistics. "But I'm not sure we can do that at the station unless the staff sergeant and Jamie have worked things out. And I'm going to be honest, I'm not sure Clyne will be thrilled with us making those calls from the station even if Jamie *is* back on the case. We'll need to go somewhere secure since we don't know who's behind the thefts. Being in a public place could work to our disadvantage. We don't want the wrong people overhearing the kinds of questions we're asking. That said, I also don't want to take you anywhere too isolated, just in case."

Her smile began to slip, and Leo felt his own hopes deflate at the same time. Why did this woman's moods have such an impact on him? But as he watched her, an idea began to form.

He had the perfect safe place to take her where she'd be surrounded by RCMP officers—protected but given the space needed to make the phone calls. And it wasn't far from their present location and, as far as he knew, on the trail route, so they wouldn't have to wander into potentially dangerous territory.

He reached across the gap between them and touched her arm. She looked at his hand and then up at him, lips parted.

For a moment, he forgot what he was going to say.

"What?" she asked, and it came back to him.

"I have an idea." He grinned at her. "How do you feel about attending a bachelor party?"

For the second time that day, Ellen followed Leo along the back trails around Schroeder Lake. He took the journey at a decent clip, careful not to exhaust the horses but also clearly aware of the time they'd already spent traveling that day. As they rode, he phoned ahead to the community center that his brothers had rented out for Sam's bachelor party and let them know that he and Ellen were on their way.

Ellen tried to focus on coming up with a clear and concise script for the phone calls to the cottage owners, but she found it difficult to stay on task. The reality of the past eighteen hours or so had begun to sink in, and her brain kept trying to dredge up the memory of Rod's final moments, intermingling them with sensory details of her mother's passing. The farther they rode, the more shallow her breathing became, and her head started to pound with a rhythm that brought dark edges to the corners of her vision.

She tried to shove it aside, to lock the memories back in place, but the assault just kept coming, fast and furious and merciless—until suddenly she felt Leo's fingers wrap around her forearm, strong pressure squeezing to remind her of the present.

"Ellen. *Ellen*."

She looked at him. His features were marked with worry.

"Are you all right? We're here. I've been trying to talk to you for the past minute or so. Where did you go? Do we need to head back to town or call a doctor?"

She shook her head, feeling the tickle of her hair on her neck. The tightness of Leo's grip. The blood pounding inside her chest. The darkness around her vision backed off, and she inhaled through her nose, filling her lungs with air. "I'm fine. Let's go inside."

Leo pressed his lips together and regarded her with mild disbelief. "You don't have to pretend with me, you know. We've known each other for a long time. If you need help, just say the word and I'll make it happen."

She nodded, knowing he spoke the truth, that he meant well—but the memories were her own battle to fight. He couldn't help her with that. No one could. Jamie had suggested several times that she talk to someone about her "moments," as he called them, but what good would that do? She'd just end up reliving her teenage years even more vividly by speaking details about her parents' deaths aloud. How could that possibly be a good thing?

"Let's go inside," she said with a little more force. "We need to start making these calls."

Leo released her arm, and to her surprise, it was as though a tiny void inside of her had opened up that she hadn't even known existed—and hadn't known could be filled—until he'd broken the connection. She thought she saw disappointment register in his eyes, too, but there was no time to dwell on that and no reason to do so. She didn't need a second big brother trying to check up on her at every turn; she had enough anxiety trying to manage Jamie's worries and occasionally obsessive concerns for her well-being.

They tied the horses up at the edge of the property inside a shed that had been transformed into a temporary stay for horses, bicycles, boats or whatever mode of transportation each group using the community center needed to house. Ellen was glad to see that Leo's brothers had pulled any potentially dangerous items out of the shed and left water and a few apples and carrots inside for the horses.

Once they were certain the animals would be all right on their own for a little while, they headed into the community center. A man Ellen didn't recognize opened the door and invited them inside. There were six men seated on couches and lounge chairs in a large meeting room, with food and drinks arranged around the periphery. A giant projector screen hung against the wall, and most of the men had game controllers in their hands.

"Leo! Ellen! Come on in." Sam bounced up from a couch and hurried over. "Have something to eat, help yourselves to soda or tea or whatever you want, please. There's a landline phone in the next room if you want to use that, or maybe you were going to use a cell? But if you want some peace and quiet while you make calls, you'd better go in there. We're playing *NHL 95*, the best hockey video game ever made. Wish you were here to play with us."

As Sam spoke, Ellen watched a sadness creep into the edges of Leo's expression, though he was trying very hard not to show it. A wave of guilt threatened to send her to her knees. This man was missing his brother's pre-wedding celebrations to play babysitter to her.

Why hadn't she just gone back to the police station? Why hadn't she left the entire investigation in the hands of the local RCMP? Yes, it had been a good idea to look around the Fosters' house, since that immediate examination of the crime scene by someone who'd just been there hadn't been an option after the other thefts, and Jamie had admitted it was helpful but…after hitting a dead end, maybe she should have let it be.

"Thanks," Leo said, clapping his brother on the back, "but the best was actually *NHL 94*, though since this is your bachelor party, I'll let it slide. And I wish I was here playing, too, but hey, it's the job."

Sam glanced at Ellen and back at Leo. "Yeah, I get it." He winked at his older brother, who looked startled at the gesture.

"It's not like that," Leo muttered, but Sam had already punched Leo in the shoulder and walked away.

Ellen's insides squeezed like a wrung-out sponge. "What does he mean? Not like what?"

Leo's sideways glance contained a hint of shyness that she couldn't recall seeing in him before. It was oddly heartwarming. "Don't worry about it. Let's get you situated and start making those calls."

The guilt pushed back to the surface. "Leo, about everything you're doing—"

"If you're going to apologize for my volunteering to become a part of this, don't. It was my decision, and if you want to discuss it further, we can do so after we've phoned around and learned something. You get started on the list, and I'm going to call Jamie and update him on where we are and what we're doing, since he's probably wondering why my GPS veered off course—oh, yep, two missed calls in the last five minutes. Hopefully the staff sergeant has cooled off a bit more and they've been able to have a reasonable discussion."

Ellen entered the side room, a small office space with a desk, several metal chairs and a phone. The room felt dark due to the cloud cover outside moving in and blocking much of the natural lighting, but she didn't mind. She'd never been a fan of turning on lights during the daytime—it had always seemed like a waste of electricity. After getting off the phone with Jamie, Leo brought the list up on his screen and set it down in front of her.

"Want me to take notes?" He opened several of the desk drawers and pulled out a

stack of old event flyers for a bonfire that
had been held at the community center three
years prior. "Just so you're aware, Jamie is
on board with having help from Fort Mason
RCMP officers on this case—yours truly,
and any of the other guys in here for that
matter—so that's not going to get him into
trouble. I'm sure you're well aware of how
my town and yours share police resources
on occasion, anyway. And it sounds like he
and the staff sergeant are patching things up.
Trucco, on the other hand, is still pretty furious, but that's not our problem right now. You
focus on speaking to the cottage owners, and
I'll write the information down. We can use
speakerphone if that's easier."

Once he'd located a pen, they sat, and Ellen
dialed the first number—but her fingers trembled as she hit each button. She fought to hold
her hand steady and hoped Leo didn't notice.
For some reason, her nerves had begun to
flare and she was having a hard time decid-
ing whether it had to do with the possibility
of finding a lead in the next few minutes, or if
it was caused by Leo's knee bumping against
hers as they sat close together in front of the
desk. Maybe it was both. Maybe it was neither.

She took a deep, grounding breath and

made the first call. No one was home. During the second call, she spoke to the owner's daughter, who suggested Ellen call back after five o'clock. The third number, however, resulted in useful information. When the owners had returned to the area for their vacation last year, they'd discovered that a piece of artwork—which they'd purchased from a local charity auction—had gone missing. The piece was valued at around twelve thousand dollars.

Local artwork, really? As Ellen replaced the phone on the cradle, she couldn't help wondering if making the calls was an exercise in futility. The staff sergeant would do all of this sooner or later, so why waste energy on it? She punched the buttons on the phone for the fourth number with extra, and unnecessary, force.

"Ellen?"

She felt Leo's eyes bore into her.

"Are you all right?"

"I'm not sure," she muttered. Someone picked up at the other end of the line as a heavy cloud passed over the community center, shrouding them in even deeper darkness. "Hello, may I speak to—"

The phone went dead. She pulled back and stared at it.

"What's wrong?" Leo sat upright. They

heard shouts of disappointment coming from the large room where the men were enjoying their party. He opened the door to a dark room, since the men had pulled the shades across the windows in order to see the projector screen better—but the screen had gone blank. Leo's older brother, Aaron, was standing up, trying the light switches.

"Power's out. We probably blew a fuse," Aaron said. "I'm surprised it didn't happen sooner. This is kind of an old building."

Ellen hung up the phone. "I thought we got cut off, but maybe it's the outage. I'll—"

The window shattered as a bang echoed through the room. A thud against the far wall caught Ellen's attention and she gasped.

A bullet sat embedded in the drywall.

The thieves had found her, and they were out for blood.

SEVEN

Ellen dove to the floor. She felt Leo's arms wrap around her back, propel her to her knees and lead her out of the small room as shouts came from the main hall. More bangs sounded in rapid succession, and the crackle of breaking glass filled the air.

Everyone dropped to the floor.

"Is someone *shooting* at us?" one of the men shouted, but the space had become so frenetic with people pushing furniture against the doors and windows that she couldn't tell who.

"It's got to be the men who went after Ellen," Leo called into the room. His grip on her tightened, keeping her from falling flat on her face. Her legs had grown wobbly, and the trembling in her hands had increased to a full shake. "They don't want you guys— they want us."

Ellen felt the zip of hot lead past her arm

and shrieked in surprise. Were these people shooting blindly into the building? Did they really want her out of the picture that badly?

"Is there a back entrance?" Leo shouted, pulling her closer to him and behind an overturned couch. It only provided cover from a few windows, though—even with the blinds pulled down, someone shooting blindly through any of the numerous windows around the common area could hit a bystander with a stray bullet.

"You can't leave!" Sam shouted back. "Are you crazy?"

"I'm the most levelheaded person in our family," Leo growled. "Trust me. I have a plan."

"Get to the basement!" Aaron called. He flipped one of the tables on its side and ducked behind it. "I've already called the police and they're on the way."

"What are you guys going to do? Shouldn't we all go down there?"

Aaron pointed at Sam and directed him with gestures to make his way to one of the windows. "Fine. Anyone who wants to get to the basement, go. Sam and I will stay here in case a perp tries to enter the building so we can meet them hand-to-hand." None of the other men moved, so Aaron began directing traffic. The men grabbed whatever they could—unbroken lamps, the mugs they'd been drinking out of, food trays—to use as weapons, each crouching next to a window in preparation for an assault.

Ellen felt like she might vomit.

Then Leo's face entered Ellen's full field of vision, stern intent written all over it. "Ellen. We need to cross the room and get down into the basement. We'll stay there until the cops arrive. Are you with me?"

She stared at him, uncomprehending. He wanted them to hide while his brothers and friends risked their lives?

"We're going on three," he said when she didn't respond. "See that door with the exit sign overhead? There's going to be a stairwell on the other side, and we're going down it."

His words hardly registered before he began to count down.

"Three…two…one…let's go!" He gripped her hand and pulled her across the room as another round of gunfire blasted through the facility. Leo slammed his fist into the door's crossbar and pulled them through, then down a short flight of stairs to a landing that led to a second flight, which curved back into the basement. But on that landing was something else: a back door.

Leo paused in front of the door. "The windows are on all the other sides of the building. We might be able to get out this way."

Ellen stared at him, incredulous. "Are you serious? You want to go out there? What happened to hiding in the basement?"

They both flinched at the sound of another window shattering.

"There are still windows in the basement, just those really small rectangular ones. And I don't know what we'll find—there might be tons of cover, or it might be open season on us for anyone who peers inside." Leo placed his hand on the crash bar of the exit. "I'm thinking we book it to the trees."

"What about the horses?" Ellen bit her lip, thinking. "It'd take time to untie them."

"Exactly. But behind this door—"

"Is the lake." Ellen gasped. "Leo, I have an idea. But we'll have to be fast, and it might be dangerous."

"More dangerous than getting shot to pieces inside a community center?" He searched her face, and warmth flooded her cheeks. "I'm out of ideas, Biers. If you've got one, lead the way."

She pressed hesitantly against the crash bar, but as soon as Leo saw what she was doing, he stepped up and took over. He opened the door a crack and peered out. When no bullets slammed into the door, he widened the crack. Ellen heard men shouting nearby, calling for the people inside the community center to just give up "the lady" and they'd go away.

"I don't see anyone," Leo said. "We're about fifteen meters from the dock, and about forty from a second dock where I see a boat. What's the next step in your plan?"

Ellen looked out the door, ducking beneath his shoulder. She saw the boat. It'd be a risk to reach either dock before the men outside the community center noticed them, but if they were quick, they'd be able to make it. Starting the boat, on the other hand, was another question entirely—but she'd honestly never known anyone in the Schroeder Lake area to take too many precautions with their boats, especially during the off-season with so few people about. Who would even be in the area to steal a boat? Plus, most folks had an easy view of their dock from the giant windows in their cottage, which overlooked the lake, similar to the giant picture windows at the Fosters' place.

Seeing the boat docked a short distance away, she had a feeling the keys would still be in the ignition—and if not, well, they'd have to cross that bridge when they came to it. Hopefully it'd be only a matter of minutes before the police arrived.

"We're going to borrow that boat." She raised her shoulders as Leo tossed her a look of alarm. "Do you have a better idea?"

He lifted his chin. "Have you looked at the sky?"

"It's either stay here and get shot, or risk being on a lake during a storm that hasn't even started yet. I'd rather put as much distance between us and these guys as possible, and maybe lead them away from your brothers and friends."

Leo's jaw tightened, but he didn't offer any resistance to her plan. Was he angry with her for destroying Sam's bachelor party and putting everyone at risk? Who was going to pay for all the damages? What if one of the guys inside made an error in judgment and got shot? What if—

"Ellen, if we're doing this, we have to go now. I don't know where you keep going, but I need you present until we're safe. Can you do that?"

She swallowed hard against the dryness in her throat. She didn't mean to keep falling into her own thoughts. It had been a long time since the memories and the guilt crept up on her—and she'd never had this many episodes, one after another. Could she guarantee she'd be able to stave them off? No, but she had to try.

Two more gunshots sounded, followed by an angry yell. The attackers were getting impatient. Ellen slipped underneath Leo's arm, which held the door open, bounced on her heels—and ran with every ounce of energy she had toward the dock.

Shelter us in Your arms, Lord. Leo bolted after Ellen, surprised at her speed and energy. She ran with perfect form and a lightness in her step that disguised the urgency of the situation. The part of his brain that was trying to keep calm recalled that Ellen had played sports in high school, but for the life of him he couldn't recall which ones. But he did remember that she'd stopped playing at some point, rather suddenly—perhaps after her father's death, when she and Jamie had to take up a lot of responsibilities at home. Particularly as their mother's mental health had begun to spiral.

Jamie had never been all that open about what happened, but Leo did know that it had taken quite a toll on Ellen, hence the overprotectiveness. If he'd grown up with a younger sister instead of two brothers, he might have been overprotective, too. Though, as the peacemaker of the Thrace siblings, he did act a *little* protective—but it had more to do with protecting their unity as a family than anything else. All brothers fought, that was normal, but Aaron and Sam had butted heads almost every day.

It had been quite the balancing act, growing up with one brother who knew exactly what he wanted out of life and one who'd figured life would just hand things to him as he needed them. Thankfully, Sam had grown up a lot over the years, and not only had he developed into a responsible, courageous RCMP officer, he was now about to marry an incredible woman who was perfect for him. As for Aaron, while he hadn't yet found someone to spend his life with, the man seemed more or less married to his job. Aaron had always been the most enthusiastic of the Thrace brothers when it came to following their father into the RCMP, and his commitment showed. Rumor had it that Aaron would be up for a significant promotion soon, which he deserved.

But with both of his brothers moving along secure paths, Leo had started to feel a little uneasy about where he fit in. He'd been so focused on himself, his career and on making sure all three Thrace brothers stayed on good terms with each other, he was starting to wonder if he'd been missing something. Like building actual relationships that held meaning and seeking value in life outside of his little bubble. He'd hoped that coming back to his childhood hometown for Sam's wedding might help to provide some perspective on things.

Not that now was the time to start. Right now, he needed to stay one step ahead of people who wanted to take his life away. It didn't take perspective to figure *that* out.

Lifting up a prayer with each step, Leo tried to keep pace with Ellen. They made it about halfway to the dock before he heard shouting behind them. They'd been spotted. Ellen's pace didn't falter, but she shifted her head as if tempted to look back.

"Don't look, keep going," he said. She redirected her focus and kept pushing, despite the sudden, loud gunshots behind them. There was something totally bizarre about the thieves having made a sudden attack during the daytime, not to mention their willingness to shoot blindly into a community center where there were other, uninvolved people present who would undoubtedly have cell phones and the ability to immediately call the police. A bloodbath certainly wouldn't help the thieves with their break-and-enter business, and if anything, it would turn up the heat over Rod's death and spur a province-wide manhunt.

What are they thinking?

Maybe they weren't, and that was the problem. Still, something about this scenario didn't sit right—but he and Ellen could parse that out once they were beyond the range of gunfire.

Ellen reached the boat and nearly dove in, keeping herself low as she made her way to the front. Leo held his breath, hoping for good news.

A split second later the engine started, and Ellen ran back onto the dock. "We have to cast off!"

Leo could have kicked himself for wasting precious seconds he could have been using to untie the boat. The men who'd shot up the community center were halfway to the dock, all of them wearing dark ball caps and red bandannas tied around their mouths. They also wore denim pants and plain black T-shirts. Definitely the same guys who'd broken into the Fosters' cottage when Ellen had been working. His fingers fumbled over the knots—and then Ellen dropped next to him, kneeling and focused. They pulled the last strand of rope free just as two of the men reached the far end of the dock.

Ellen jumped back into the boat, and Leo followed behind. He braced himself for gunfire as one man raised his weapon, but Ellen gave the boat gas and the watercraft burst forward. Leo lost his footing and fell onto the padded passenger seats.

"Are you okay?" Ellen called over her shoulder.

Leo pushed himself upright, rattled but unharmed. "I'm all right. Are you? Do you know how to steer this thing?"

"Sort of. Not particularly. A little bit?" She glanced back at him, but her eyes almost immediately slipped past and found the dock. Her lips parted in surprise as her forehead creased. "Uh, Leo?"

Worry seized his gut. He twisted around to look. Several of the armed thieves had made their way farther down the shoreline to the next cottage's dock and were stealing a boat of their own.

A lump formed in Leo's throat. Wilderness, he could deal with. Problems on land, he could handle. But boats? Even during his childhood, the Thrace family hadn't spent much time on Schroeder Lake, and when they had, it was in little self-propelled kay-aks or canoes, not high-powered motorboats. He didn't even swim all that well, and hadn't been in the water for years.

"Can we beat them across the lake? Or, I don't know, circle around and lead them back to the community center? The police should arrive at any second."

Ellen pressed her lips together and turned back to the steering wheel. Rudder? Leo had no idea what the different parts of the boat were called, or how fast different types of boats could go. As their enemies came closer, Ellen gave the engine more gas. Leo didn't miss how her hands tightened around the steering wheel, knuckles growing white as tension pushed her shoulders up around her ears.

He reached out to rest his hand on her hip, not wanting to interfere with her steering or focus but aching to offer reassurance. "Ellen, you're doing fantastic. I know you're feel-ing unsure about your skill here, but you're far better at it than I could possibly be. I can barely cut an oar through the water properly, let alone pilot a giant speedboat like this."

"Cuddy cabin," she said, her voice flat and matter-of-fact. "It's called a cuddy cabin, which means there's not a real below-decks to speak of, just enough room in the little berth to sleep and use the washroom."

"You know a lot about boats?" He noticed how her shoulders started to relax the longer she talked. He risked a glance back at their pursuers. He and Ellen still had a decent lead, but the thieves were gaining on them bit by bit. "A little more gas, Ellen. I know we're going really, really fast. But you have control, I can tell."

Her right eye twitched at the word *control*, which he filed away for later. His words had touched a nerve, but without hesitation, she increased the speed. Leo's heart pounded against his ribs. The speed they were traveling felt uncomfortable enough for him as a passenger, and with that last burst of power, the boat seemed to have taken on a life of its own. The wheel shook and tried to pull out from Ellen's grasp.

"You've got this. You're doing so well, Ellie."

She gasped and released the wheel. It was only a split second, less than a fraction of a moment before she grabbed it again, but it was enough. The boat jerked to the left, sending them careening toward the shore at a terrifying speed. Ellen struggled to pull it back the other way, to right their course, but something had affected her and she was having trouble getting them back on track.

Leo leaped from his seat and stood behind her, wrapping his arms around her body from behind to grip the steering wheel above both of her hands. "Tell me what to do," he said, trying not to shout into her ear, though it was difficult to hear anything above the whine of the engine grinding at near max capacity.

A gunshot sounded off the stern. A quick glance back told him that their pursuers weren't much closer yet, but had clued in that there might be a way to rattle them again. If Ellen lost control of the boat a second time at this speed, they risked crashing into a dock or even into one of the boat sheds along the shore. The end result would be nothing short of deadly.

God, guide her hands.

"They're coming up pretty quickly behind us. Here's an idea—what if we veer to the right and double back? We can keep our distance from the gunshots, but it'll take the guy driving the boat a few seconds to follow suit. It might give us a lead to get back to shore." He risked another glance at their pursuers, praying that at any moment he'd see red-and-blue lights approaching the community center behind them.

"Starboard," Ellen said.

"What?"

"Starboard." She leaned to the right and guided the wheel. Leo leaned into it with her, helping to control the steering, keeping his grip gentle but firm. "The right side of a boat is starboard."

He felt her body lose the slightest bit of tension when she spoke. "How do you know all this boat stuff? You'll have to tell me about it when we're back." He checked the water behind them as their boat made the turn. The cuddy cabin took the turn quite wide, but at the speed they were going, if they attempted the maneuver any faster or made sharp movements, they'd risk capsizing. They were already having enough issues keeping the watercraft steady, and the last thing he and Ellen needed was to be pitched into the water at the direct mercy of the men with guns. Especially since he couldn't really swim.

Once they'd completed their 180-degree turn to head back to shore, their boat was seconds away from drawing alongside the boat driven by the thieves. Leo stiffened. He and Ellen would have to brace themselves and duck, momentarily taking their eyes off the water, but better that than risk a bullet.

"All right, Ellen, we need to get down in three, two—wait, what are they doing?"

He wanted to yell. They couldn't catch a break.

Instead of making the turn as he and Ellen had and following the cuddy cabin boat back to shore, the thieves did exactly what Leo had been too cautious to attempt. The man at the helm yanked the wheel to the right well before reaching Leo and Ellen's boat, sending the thieves' boat into a sideways skid on the water. Leo watched with helplessness as one of the men aboard lost his balance and went careening overboard, landing in the water with a splash.

All too quickly, the driver corrected the boat's balance and regained its forward momentum.

The driver gunned the engine, sending his stolen boat on a collision course headed straight toward them.

EIGHT

"Ellen?" Leo's voice was urgent in her ear. She didn't miss the underlying tension in his attempted show of calm. She also didn't miss the boat that was heading directly for them.

"I see it," she said. "I have an idea."

Whether the idea would work or was even plausible, she didn't know. Technically speaking, she didn't know how to drive a motorboat, either, but Leo had seemed even more clueless than her, and his confidence in her had given her the courage to keep going.

Until he'd called her by the nickname she hadn't heard since the day her mother died.

"Care to share?" In her peripheral vision, she saw Leo's head swing back and forth, between the boat and the shore they were headed for. It was too far and too risky to try putting on more speed. They were already traveling dangerously fast, and there was no telling whether their pursuer was crazy enough to increase his boat's speed, too.

So she did the opposite.

"Hold on tight," she told Leo.

Then she slammed on the brake at the same moment the driver of the other boat abandoned ship and dove into the water.

The other boat zipped past their bow, so close that Ellen could make out the dents and scratches in its paint.

The instant it passed by, she kicked the cuddy cabin into high gear again, racing toward the shore and the community center. Two more masked men were standing at the edge of the water, pointing their weapons at the lake.

At least they're smart enough not to fire when we're so close to their own crew, she thought.

"The thieves' boat is going to crash in about three seconds. No, don't look," Leo said. "Uh-oh. It's going to hit someone's boat shed." She appreciated the notice, and though it was tempting to risk a glance, she stayed focused despite the sound of a heavy object slamming into a wooden structure. Boards cracked and metal crunched, but she refused to be swayed.

She'd planned to zip back up to the community center dock, but with the other armed thieves standing right on the shore, there was no way.

"We're going to have to run for it," she said, the realization making her stomach sick. She looked at the fuel gauge in the boat. They'd expended almost the entire tank with their high-speed flight around the lake, and letting the fuel run out would make them sitting ducks. Landing the boat elsewhere would also mean potentially wandering into a dangerous situation—what if the thieves had cars and could then just follow and nab them? At least they had one form of transportation left, and it went where cars couldn't follow.

Rumblings of thunder overhead also told her it was time to get off the lake, lest the situation become doubly unsafe.

"Pull up at the dock on the other side of the community center," Leo suggested. "It's closer to the edge of the property where the horses are tethered. It'll be tight, but we don't exactly have another option."

Her thoughts exactly. She tried to keep her breathing steady as she slowed the boat, but not too much. She kept them going fast enough that the moment the cuddy cabin came alongside the shore, she and Leo leaped over the side onto the dock and sprinted toward the shed.

Angry shouting grew closer as the thieves also raced to reach them. Bangs split the air.

"Are they shooting again? With horses nearby?" She wanted to scream. Maybe they weren't so smart, after all.

The instant they reached the shed, she and Leo vaulted onto the horses, gripped the reins and burst back out again. Air rushed past Ellen's face as another bang sounded, and she gasped as the sound made her head spin, her vision blurring as the darkness started to encroach...

"Focus, Ellen! Focus!" Leo's shouting brought her back to the present. They galloped across the community center property and veered onto the narrow trail. The shouts of their pursuers grew quieter as the distance between them increased.

When the loudest sound around them was the continued deep rumble of thunder overhead, they slowed the horses. Leo looked over his shoulder at her, then slowed further until they rode alongside each other.

"Are you okay? How are you holding up?"

She shrugged. She honestly wasn't sure. Anxiety gnawed at her insides now that the adrenaline rush had begun to fade, and a sense of hopelessness had begun to pervade her thoughts.

"We're going to be all right," Leo said, though his voice sounded as shaky as she felt. "If they'd followed us, we'd have heard them by now. I'm going to get Jamie on the phone and tell him to send some uniforms out to the community center—oh, hang on, he's calling right now."

Jamie's voice came through loud and clear on the speaker the second Leo answered. "What just happened? Are you two all right? I got a call from inside the community center. Apparently there were shots fired and—"

"We're fine," Ellen said, though she wasn't entirely sure she believed her own statement.

Leo smiled at her gently, as if he knew—and for some reason or another, she felt a flush of warmth run through her. "Ellen's quick thinking saved us. Literally saved us. Thank You, God."

The warm flush disappeared. She looked away, staring anywhere but at Leo and the phone.

"Don't say that around Ellen," Jamie quipped. "She snaps at me whenever I bring God up."

"*Jamie.* Not the time." She didn't miss the questioning glance from Leo. Yes, they all used to attend youth group together, and their families had been members of the same church in Fort St. Jacob. No, she didn't want to talk about it right now.

Jamie sighed. Ellen felt the weight of it, the disappointment that radiated from him even through the phone line, now that he'd been assured of her safety and lack of injury. "This whole business has gone too far. Clyne and I talked things over and he's on board with taking this investigation more seriously—by which I mean listening to other people as well as Trucco, instead of letting her push everyone else around. Clyne knew Rod, too. Everyone did, and the people in town want justice. I made my case for letting you inside, and he understands that time was of the essence. He admitted that he'd probably have done the same thing in my situation. I showed him the cigarette butt, too, but we've given that to Trucco for testing and we're pulling Hogan in for questioning."

"That's a relief." Leo squeezed Ellen's shoulder. When he let go, she wished he'd held on longer. And then she wished that she wasn't having those kinds of thoughts at such a critically serious time. "Let me guess, he wants us to step back now, though? We learned one small thing from the phone calls, but it may be helpful. Someone else should take over making the rest of the calls. I really do think it's a viable method to start getting some answers and making connections between the break-ins. Hopefully Trucco can get some information from the cigarette butt. It feels important, somehow."

"I agree." Jamie cleared his throat and sniffed. "Hey, Leo, can you pass the phone to Ellen for a sec? I want to talk to her directly—family business."

"No problem." Leo turned off speakerphone and handed over the device. "I'll be a few meters away, okay?"

She watched him saunter off, then turned her attention to Jamie. "What is it? I'm fine. You don't need to worry about me. It would have been helpful if the police had made it to the lake in time, but—"

"Ellen. Hold up. I was going to talk to you about this back at the station, but since I'm not sure when you'll get here…" Jamie's sharp tone of voice brought her back to focus.

She had no idea where he was going with this. "Really, what?"

Jamie paused before plunging ahead. "It's about Leo. He's my friend, sis, but he's RCMP. It's hard enough that I have to spend day in and day out worrying what will happen to you if anything happens to me, but getting romantically involved with an officer… especially after Mom…"

She lowered her voice. "Leo and I? We're not romantically involved. We're not anything involved."

Jamie chuckled without humor. "Is he sure of that? When he called me a little earlier about making the phone calls to the other victims…there was something in the way he talked about you and said your name. Trust me, it would have been impossible to miss. I've known the guy for a very long time."

Ellen blinked rapidly, unsure how to respond to her brother's insinuation. Of course nothing was going on between her and Leo, even if her childhood crush on him had somehow returned and manifested into a grown-up respect, appreciation and, yes, attraction. But she was the little kid, the younger sister, the friend-by-proxy. She had zero expectation of Leo ever seeing her as anything else.

Jamie finally sighed. "Just be careful, okay?"

She managed to extricate herself from the phone call, but her cheeks felt like they were on fire. She was very glad Leo hadn't overheard *that* conversation on speakerphone. When she trotted back up to Leo to hand over his phone, she noticed a flashing text message notification.

"Looks like your brothers are trying to talk to you? I thought I heard a call-waiting beep, but I wasn't sure."

Leo took the phone back and grinned at her as he opened up the text app. "Good talk with your brother?"

Was her face *that* red? That was what she got for having such a pale complexion—but despite herself, her heart gave another tiny hop inside her chest, thanks to his smile. Even if she had growing feelings for Leo, even if she'd noticed—in the midst of life-or-death danger on the lake—how perfectly his arms had fit around her and how well she'd tucked up against him as he helped steer, he'd never feel the same way. Her heart needed to calm down and take a reality check.

Leo's grin vanished as soon as he read his text messages. "Huh."

"What is it?" Her chest tightened with anticipation. She couldn't tell if his reaction was good or bad.

"Well, this might be good news, but I'm not sure." He looked up at her, brow furrowed. "Aaron dug one of the bullets out of the wall after the shooters backed off. Ellen, those guys weren't trying to kill everyone in the community center at all. They were trying to draw you out. The attack was very strategic. This isn't normal ammunition we're looking at. They were using *rubber* bullets."

The shock and surprise reflected on Ellen's face mirrored Leo's own. According to Aaron's text, one of Sam's friends had also been hit by a stray bullet, and while he had a massive, painful welt on his abdomen, he was otherwise all right. Doug's injury and Aaron's initial finding prompted the rest of the guys to help take a closer look at the holes in the walls of the community center. Only some of the walls were plastered, with the lowest level being merely painted-over concrete. It meant that bullets hadn't done much more than bounce around in the basement.

Trucco is going to have a field day with this.

"But they tried to kill us with the boat," Ellen said, incredulous. "We almost didn't make it."

Leo reached across the small space between them, gripped her shoulder and squeezed. "I know. Consider that it happened after we were outside of the community center, though. I have a feeling they were firing real bullets at us on the water. Look, whoever is organizing these events isn't keen on unnecessary loss of life. And this fits the modus operandi of these thieves, in a way. Rod's death was an accident. You seeing it happen was unexpected. Your presence means their operation is at risk, so now they want to eliminate you from the equation but without bringing down too much heat onto themselves."

Ellen swept her arm from one side to the other. "And of course, nobody saw them. Even though they were firing weapons in broad daylight. The location, the time of year, the weather… What I can't figure out is how they knew I was there."

That had been eating at Leo, too. "I'd say maybe they drove past on the way to another break-in and saw us go inside, or maybe they saw the horses tied up and are aware that we've been using RCMP animals to get around. I'd suggest Hogan could have even told them, but Jamie said someone was bringing him in for questioning, right?"

Ellen shrugged. "But he could have told someone before we arrived."

"I'm calling Jamie back." Something nagged at the back of Leo's mind. They were missing a critical piece of information, and it felt just out of reach. As soon as the call reconnected, he blurted out his question. "Who else knew we were here?"

Jamie, to his credit and Leo's relief, responded with grace. "Honestly? Half the detachment. I was meeting with the staff sergeant and a few other officers when your call came in, and we all had a quick briefing about what we were each going to do next. Unless one of the other officers spoke to someone outside the station—or one of them mentioned it over the radio—then I hate to say it, but we'll have to suspect the worst."

"Isn't it reasonable that the people responsible for the break-ins have a police scanner?" Ellen suggested. "To listen in on local communications? That would give them a way to make sure there were no police in the area before a break-in."

Leo nodded thoughtfully. "Actually, that makes a lot of sense. Either they've got a police scanner or the leak came from inside. Neither option is a good one."

Ellen groaned and tilted her head back, exposing the smooth skin of her neck to the cloudy sky. Leo looked away before she caught him staring.

"I was actually just about to call back and suggest that you two head back to the station," Jamie said. "Now I'm not so sure."

Leo rubbed his chin. "We'll be surrounded by a multitude of officers, and I assume there are cameras in most of the rooms?" Jamie confirmed there were. "I'll make sure we spend time in public areas and stay in rooms with security monitoring. Just in case. I'm sure there's a reasonable explanation for this—and the police scanner idea makes the most sense. We'll meet you there?"

"We'll keep going down these trails and head back to the far end of the pasture, so we bring the horses in the same way we left," Ellen chimed in. She began to massage the back of her neck with one hand. Leo regretted not being back at the station already, or else he'd offer to do it for her. That boat trip had to have left her painfully tense all over, with a headache soon to follow if she wasn't nursing one already. "You were right about the route, Jamie. The entire time we've been on these, we haven't seen a single person. I mean, the thieves know we're on them now, but they're getting around in cars and we're moving quickly. It's not like they can bring cars into the forest, and as long as we keep this pace, they're unlikely to catch up on foot."

"Keep going, then," Jamie said. "Before it starts to rain. I'm glad you're both alive, by the way."

Leo tucked his phone away and they continued, driving the horses at a decent clip. After riding for several minutes, Leo slowed his horse's pace again until Ellen and her horse drew up parallel.

"Are you sure you're all right?" Her complexion had turned paler than usual, and her lively hair looked more like a tangled mess than a regal mane. Her hands gripped the reins with almost as much intensity as she'd held the steering wheel on the boat. When she nodded without meeting his eyes, he reached out to touch her hand.

She flinched and her gaze snapped to the side, eyes wide and wild, rosy lips parted.

He winced at her expression. "Sorry, I didn't mean to startle you. I just… What happened back there was super intense and terrifying. I know I've said it a thousand times by now, but you're allowed to be upset. I'm still quaking like jelly inside. Praise God that the bullets at the community center were rubber and no one got badly hurt. And He was definitely looking out for us on the water. When that boat came at us, I didn't think we were going to make it. By God's grace—"

"Will you *stop that* already?"

He froze. The horse stopped moving beneath him. "Excuse me?"

Ellen stopped, too, and twisted in the saddle to piece his heart with eyes like daggers. "Stop it. Stop talking about God's grace or mercy or whatever you claim happened out there. God didn't save us. My quick thinking and your experience did. Coincidence and good timing played a part. If God is even real, He definitely doesn't care enough to save anyone's life, because if He did—"

Her words were cut off as she snapped her lips shut. Muscles around her mouth and eyes began to tic, and she whipped back around, nudging the horse into motion without another word.

A deep ache formed in the pit of Leo's stomach, because he had a feeling he knew what she would have said next. How hadn't he seen it before? Why hadn't Jamie said anything about Ellen's struggles with faith before?

If she wasn't clearly so dead set against having a discussion about it right now, he'd love to talk with her and get her side of the story. The young Ellen he knew had loved youth group and been actively involved in the church's community outreach activities, and had sung along to the hymns and choruses with passion and earnest devotion on Sunday mornings. Jamie had been the Biers sibling more likely to sleep in and miss the service.

Leo's heart hurt for her, and the force of his emotions caught him by surprise. He tried to tell himself that it had everything to do with their being childhood friends and nothing to do with the way his mind could easily picture the two of them sitting in a church pew together on a Sunday morning, a little one by their side. Or standing in the kitchen, cooking dinner together—his arms wrapped around her the same way he'd held her on the boat— stirring a pot of soup, stealing kisses every time she turned her head, curls tickling his nose...

Whoa, buddy. Come back to earth. She sees you as her brother's friend and nothing more, and besides, you made a promise to Jamie a long time ago to never become romantically involved with her.

Leo knew it was hard enough for Jamie to go to work every day not knowing if he'd come home—which was the reality for any law enforcement professional—but Jamie never, ever wanted his sister to endure the same kind of heartbreak and loss as their mother had. And after his mother's spiral into depression and eventual passing, Jamie had been even more certain that Ellen had too much of their mother in her. Jamie had expressed to Leo that he didn't want to see the same thing happen to Ellen, and Leo couldn't blame him for that at all. Ellen was his friend, too, and he'd never be able to forgive himself if *he* was the cause of her darkness and sorrow.

And maybe someday he'd have a conversation with her about faith and God's grace. But for now, he needed to get her back to the station and secured until the men who'd tried to kill her could be arrested and hauled off the streets.

He pressed his heels into his horse to return to Ellen's side, only to feel stray drops of rain hit his face.

Ellen looked back at him again. "Did you feel that, too, or am I imagining it?"

"I thought maybe I'd imagined it, but look at the path—those look like drops to me." As soon as the words left his mouth, the skies opened up. The droplets became a steady rain, and as both he and Ellen increased their horses' pace toward town, the rain became a downpour.

Within thirty seconds, they'd gone from droplets to heavy, intense rain that transformed their small trail from dusty path to slippery, muddy swampland.

"Do you think we should find the road?" Ellen called to him above the torrential din. "It's getting hard to see."

Leaving the shelter of the trail meant risking higher visibility on the road...but staying on the trail meant risking the horses' footing. And considering how much they'd slowed since the rain had started, using the muddy trail would make the journey back to town that much longer.

"It'll be faster on the road and less dangerous for the horses, but I'm concerned about your safety."

But even as he spoke, he felt his horse's weight shift beneath him. A section of muddy path sloughed away into the small ditch beside the trail, and the horse gave a nervous grunt. If one of their horses was injured, that would present just as much of a problem, because he refused to send Ellen back to town by herself. It'd make her an even greater potential target, but neither would he want her to remain on the trail all alone.

Ellen gestured at the path. "We have to get back to the road. It's too dangerous here."

He didn't like it, but he agreed with her. They plunged into the trees, but it soon became apparent that finding the road again was another challenge entirely. The trek took them through a half kilometer of wild, dense forest, and by the time they made it through—with only a few stumbles—and finally clattered onto the road, much of the force of the rain had eased.

"How much farther until we reach town?" Ellen asked. She shook out one of her arms, sending water drops flying. They were both drenched from head to toe, and the horses weren't faring much better.

"Ten minutes, maybe." He ran a hand through his hair, trying to stop water from dripping into his face. "Maybe I should call ahead and tell the guys at the station to order in some soup and hot chocolate. And some towels."

"And a change of clothes. Jamie can run to our place and grab something for both of us to wear."

"That's not a bad idea. Hang on, I need to pause for a second so I can dig the phone out of my pocket. Good thing these new smartphones are water resistant."

They stopped as Leo reached into his saturated denim to pull out the phone.

"Hey, we should move farther off to the side," Ellen said as he unlocked the screen. "There's a car coming."

"Good idea." The car came closer as Leo

brought up Jamie's number and pressed the call button. The car seemed to be driving a little fast for how wet the roads were, but Leo suspected law enforcement had similar issues with drivers in and around Fort St. Jacob as his team did up in Fort Mason. The long straightaways tended to tempt drivers into ignoring the speed limits and driving too fast, despite the risks involved with traveling at high speeds in an area known for having a high deer and moose population. Hitting a deer was dangerous, but it was possible to walk away from that type of impact. Hitting a moose, on the other hand… The percentage of fatalities from moose collisions made high speeds in moose country incredibly risky.

The phone call connected and Jamie picked up.

"Hey, you two get caught in the rain? I'm running over to our place to grab a change of clothes for you both and some microwave soup packets. How far are you from the station?"

"About ten minutes or so, faster if we pick up the pace and push the horses the rest of the way, which I'm considering." Leo glanced up and frowned. The approaching car hadn't slowed at all, and the horses had begun to shift with unease. "We'll just have to—"

"Watch out!" Ellen shouted. Leo looked up as the car swerved onto the road's shoulder.

The speeding car was heading straight for them.

NINE

The car tires crunched on the unpaved shoulder. The horses, terrified by the giant metal monster barreling toward them, bucked as the vehicle zipped past in an intentional sideswipe. Leo felt his body leave the saddle, and the phone flew from his hand as his arms pinwheeled in an attempt to correct his position—but he didn't make it. He slammed into the ground on his back. Pain, sharp and blinding, shot up his spine and into his left elbow. All he wanted to do was close his eyes and curl up on the ground, but if his horse had bucked him, surely Ellen's had done the same.

He tried to see through the sparks in his vision, and his stomach sank to see Ellen lying in the ditch, curled into the fetal position. *Please, Lord. Let her be all right.*

Before he gathered the strength to call to her, she moved. She raised her head and looked toward the horses. They were stamping and shaking their heads, eyes wide. He and Ellen needed to get to them before they decided to take off on their own.

"Are you all right?" Ellen shouted. "Leo?"

He had to try twice before he was able to take a full enough breath to respond. "I'm not sure, but we don't have time to take stock of it right now. We need to get control of the horses before—"

The sound of a car engine revving shot panic into his insides. He wished he was only imagining it, but no—the driver was definitely coming back for a second pass, and both he and Ellen were lying vulnerable on the ground. He had a feeling that if the driver was armed, that person wouldn't be using rubber bullets this time.

"Ellen, can you stand? We need to get the horses and get out of here."

His vision was still hazy, but he watched her get to her feet and bolt up the steep ditch to where her horse anxiously paced on the shoulder. Through pure force of will, he followed suit and reached his horse just in time to grab the reins, swing himself up and get the animal moving. The car zoomed toward them a second time.

"Back into the woods!" Leo shouted to Ellen as the car swerved onto the shoulder again. Before they could tell the horses what to do, the animals both bolted toward the tree line as if on the same page as their riders. Once they were deep enough into the trees that the road was no longer visible, Leo instructed his horse to stop. "Ellen, hang on. We need to figure out what we're doing."

She pulled her horse to a stop, too, and waited as he came alongside her.

"I don't know if anyone got out of the car to follow us, so we should keep moving. But I'm not sure what the best course of action is. The trail is muddy, and going back to the road isn't an option in case they're waiting."

Ellen groaned. "Great. How did they even know we were there? Why can't we catch a break?"

"If I had an answer to that, we'd have a much better idea of who's behind all this, I suspect."

"Can you call Jamie?" She pointed at his pocket. "Ask him to come out and pick us up. I'm sure once the car driver sees a patrol car heading their way, they'll back off."

"Good idea." Leo reached into his pocket. It was empty. He groaned as he remembered why. "But not possible. I dropped it when the horse bucked. It's back by the side of the road, and there's no guarantee it's even in one piece anymore. Either one of the horses might have stepped on it, or the car could have run clean over it."

Ellen's face fell. "Great. Just great."

"At least it's not pouring rain now." He shrank at the withering glare she shot him. "I know, I know. It's not much. We'll figure something out."

"If you're about to tell me that the Lord provides, keep it to yourself."

He had been about to say a variation on the theme, but her comment ruled *that* out. What could he say that wouldn't cause all the inner pain she carried around to come flooding out? He wanted to encourage her, to reassure her that they'd find a way back to town, that they'd be fine without their position being monitored via GPS and that the police would get the case solved sooner rather than later, but he wasn't sure if he believed the latter part of that. Of course God was looking out for them; he believed that with his whole heart, but all the phrases that came to mind seemed too trite or sounded to his ears like he'd be putting down her struggle. The last thing he wanted to say was something that took away from the reality of what she'd been through. Grief took many forms, and not recognizing that or refusing to accept it would be wrong.

Instead, he said the only thing that seemed right. "I hear you, Ellen. And I'm here for you if you want to talk about it. And even if you don't."

Her features softened. "Thanks."

They continued walking the horses through the trees, but they had to step carefully in the dense wilderness and the partially obscured forest floor. A great deal of plant growth on the forest floor was lovely to look at, but made it difficult for the horses to see where they were stepping, presenting a whole other problem. After several minutes of silence, Ellen sighed heavily, but said nothing.

"Are you okay?" He didn't want to pry, especially after leaving the invitation open for her, but her eyes looked unfocused, as if deep in thought. "If you have one, any idea will help, even if it seems unusual."

"It's not that it's unusual, it's more...potentially uncomfortable. I was thinking we could head west, back toward the lake, to the cottage nearest to where we are right now. I clean two places at the southernmost tip of Schroeder Lake, and I could get us inside to use the phone. Jamie could bring one of the trailers for the horses so we can get a proper ride back without risking the road again. Or he could have some officers come to ride the horses back to town and give us a lift. I don't know. It's a huge hassle, I realize, and I'm not scheduled to clean those places for another few weeks—right before the owners come back—but I'm sure they wouldn't be opposed to us using a phone during an emergency. It just means picking through the forest for a bit longer, unless we wanted to risk the sludgy trail going back. But the nearest cottage isn't far. Maybe five minutes directly that way."

Staying in the forest wasn't ideal, but what other choice did they have? And five minutes on a direct route in order to call for help sounded a whole lot more appealing than getting run down on the road.

"Are you sure? I have no doubt the RCMP can explain everything to the homeowners if there's an issue."

"I'm more concerned about our survival and keeping these horses from injury than I am getting fired from a cleaning job," she said. "And yes, I'd let the police handle any questions after the fact."

After the fact. After this was all said and done, after the local detachment had rounded up the thieves and arrested them for theft and homicide. After Leo had already returned to

Fort Mason and gotten back into the busy rhythm of his own job, far away from Ellen. Why was it that although they were only hours away from each other, he hadn't seen her for years and years?

Well, that wasn't entirely true. He'd seen her in passing now and again. But he hadn't really *looked*. At least not the way he looked at her now—in a way that warmed him from the inside out. That made him want to submit a transfer request to a certain town a few hours south of Fort Mason.

Would he really be willing to leave his brothers for a woman? For love?

I'm not in love, and I need to stop that train of thought before it even leaves the station. I made a promise to a friend, and these last few days have shown me how right he was to ask it of me.

Leo needed to give up any thoughts of Ellen that weren't immediately conducive to getting her to safety—because she was still in jeopardy and would continue to be until he found her a way back to the police station and the watchful eyes of her brother.

He suppressed everything that wasn't related to the current situation and cleared his throat.

"In that case, lead the way."

* * *

Curious. In a matter of minutes, Leo's tone of voice had changed from concerned friend to matter-of-fact RCMP officer. She wasn't sure whether to be relieved or worried by the shift. She swallowed down her compulsion to ask him about it and focused on helping her horse pick his way across the dense forest floor instead. She still couldn't believe how easily Leo had backed off after her request not to talk about "God things"—she'd expected him to launch into a diatribe or a patronizing lecture based on sentiments she'd long since rejected.

When he'd respected her words instead, her heart had melted. Just a little bit.

A little bit more *than it already has*, she reminded herself. *But his words came from a place of friendship and familiarity, nothing else. I need to stop reading into it.*

"It's not much farther," she said, seeing a break between the trees. A green backyard peeked through tree trunks ahead—and then she noticed movement, like something dashing between the trees. She held back her gasp, wondering if maybe it had been a deer. Then she heard rustling from another nearby dense crop of growth. A sinking sensation filled her stomach and she turned back to Leo. He sat frozen in the saddle. "Should we…?"

He nodded sharply and shifted to get his horse moving again—but before the animals took more than a few steps, three men with black ball caps and red bandannas tied around their faces slipped out from the trees. Two of them blocked the way forward, and one shifted around behind Ellen and Leo on the path.

"You shouldn't," said one. He raised a gun at them, and the other two followed suit.

In front of her, Leo slowly raised his hands. Ellen took a cue from him and did the same, though what she really wanted to do was kick the horses into high gear and bowl these people over. However, that wouldn't be wise—not with guns in play. Risking their own lives and those of the highly trained police horses wasn't worth it.

"Off the horses," growled the same man. "Keep your hands where we can see them."

Ellen's stomach churned. Was there a chance they could make a break for it into the trees? She glanced at Leo, who shook his head ever so slightly. If he didn't deem it safe, she didn't want to try it.

As they dismounted, the horses began to shift nervously. Ellen stroked Boomer's flank, murmuring to the creature, but one of the armed men reached between the horses and grabbed her arm, pulling her forward.

"Up where we can see you," he snarled.

Ellen gaped. "What, do you think I'm making sneak attack plans with the horse?"

"Ellen." Leo's tone held a note of warning.

She swallowed down her next volley of angry retorts, knowing Leo was right. Antagonizing these men was about the worst thing they could do. They needed to buy themselves some time and figure out a way to contact the RCMP again. She hoped that Jamie was already out searching for them. When Leo's phone was smashed, Jamie would only have their last known coordinates on the phone-finder app to go on, but at least it would give him a starting point. She didn't think they were *that* far from where they'd been run off the road.

Pinpricks of fear needled her insides as the thieves shoved her and Leo in front of the horses, forcing them to walk in between two of the armed men as they headed away from the clearing and deeper into the forest. The men held their weapons at the ready, as if they expected to use them at any moment. It looked strange to Ellen—the men appeared not very comfortable holding the deadly devices, more like people posing with an object because they thought it made them look cool.

She slid her gaze over to Leo, trying to communicate through gestures at the weapons. *Are those filled with rubber bullets, too?* But he only shook his head again and kept walking.

"Where are we going?" she asked. "My brother is in the RCMP, and this man is an officer. The detachment will know we're missing if we don't report in with them in the next five minutes. Thanks to you guys, our whereabouts are being monitored, so—"

One of the men chuckled, and the sound sent a shiver down Ellen's spine. "Is that so? With what? This smashed phone?" The man pulled a flattened phone with a shattered screen out of his pocket and laughed. "Fat chance of that."

Leo offered her a sympathetic smile. She'd tried and failed to bluff the thieves. Now she just felt sick.

His fingers found hers as the thieves ushered them through the forest. The warmth and strength he lent her as he squeezed her hand almost gave her hope that he had a plan, but when they broke through the trees and onto the lawn, a strange feeling washed over Ellen. She knew this vacation cottage, too.

The dropping temperature of late afternoon had caused the freshly dropped rainwater to evaporate and give rise to a misty ground fog. It gave the property's exterior an eerie look, though Ellen knew very well that the house's interior was painted in white and pastel yellow, and that the owners collected beaver-themed knickknacks. Many of the rooms inside resembled the retail shelves for tourists at local shops. A house didn't get much *less* threatening than that.

The door swung open as they were marched up the steps. Another man with a black ball cap and a red bandanna tied around his nose and mouth appeared at the door. His eyes narrowed at Ellen and Leo, then took in their armed escorts.

"It's about time." He stepped back, calling into the house. Ellen noticed that he wore gloves. "Hey, boys! We've got company. For a little while, at least."

For a little while.

Ellen hadn't missed the implication. They'd been captured and brought to the site of a robbery in progress.

No one knew where they were.

They'd become prisoners of the very people who'd been eagerly trying to kill them.

TEN

"Move," the man said, waving his gun as though it were a toy. Then he addressed their armed escort. "You two, take the horses out back."

Ellen's limbs refused to move. Her brain told her that the safest thing to do right now was cooperate, to keep these men calm while she and Leo thought up a way to escape. But her body had other ideas, and it wasn't keen on being trapped inside a building with a bunch of armed thieves who'd killed her friend and had been doing their best to ensure she met the same fate.

"Let's go, Ellen," Leo murmured. "We're going to figure this out."

His words weren't all that reassuring, because as the man who'd opened the door stepped aside for them to enter, she saw two other men walking around the living room and heard more thumps coming from the upper floor. Just like what had happened at the Fosters' place. And now they were going to be killed, too, just like Rod, and—

"Breathe, Ellen. Through your nose. Slowly." Leo's hand touched the small of her back and guided her forward. She tried to control her breathing, but darkness hovered at the edges of her vision again and threatened to take over. If she collapsed here and now, that would be it. They'd easily dispose of her without resistance. She needed to stay upright and alert.

"We're going inside the clean house," Leo continued. "You do a great job cleaning these places, there's hardly any dust collected on the surfaces."

Why was he talking about housecleaning at a time like this? If they were killed in here, it'd just make a huge mess anyway, and—

Oh. She inhaled sharply. They were *inside* the house, and if the men wanted to make use of those illegal handguns they were waving around, there was no way they'd shoot her and Leo inside the house. It'd be messy, risky and would undoubtedly result in blood spatter on themselves, too—making the identity of the thieves that much easier to figure out. The men would have to dispose of their clothes somehow *and* find a way to wash the blood off without being seen by anyone or leaving evidence behind. Yes, there were ways to do all of these things, but it added extra variables, which meant much greater room for error. And for thieves who relied on stealth and hidden identities to get the job done, making a mess would be unwise.

"What are we gonna do with them?" one of the other masked men growled. "Why didn't you just shoot 'em outside?"

The man who'd led them into the house snorted. "Without the go-ahead? You want to have that conversation?"

"We been working hard enough to get rid of the lady already. Ain't that approval enough? Why we gotta wait for some kind of green light?"

Someone shoved Ellen hard in the back, barking instructions. "I said *move!*"

She stumbled over her steps, but Leo's hand remained glued to her at all times. It felt more and more comforting to have him physically connected to her, the deeper they were drawn into the cottage.

"Boss has a plan for how things are to be done. Putting a bullet through their skulls on private property isn't part of the plan. They were supposed to be taken care of out on the road, and since that didn't happen, the instructions I got were to just track them down so we can finish the job without interruption. Where else are we supposed to stash them until boss gives us the green light to get rid of them?"

One of the men raised his arms over his head and turned from side to side, attempting to appeal to his fellow thieves. "They were also supposed to be taken care of out on the water. And outside the center. But none of those worked, did they? And now we've got a lawman here with us listening to every word. You ever think that maybe none of those attempts have been successful because the boss is just really bad at coming up with a plan? Huh? I say we take 'em out back and put one through their chests. No complications, less mess, done. No one the wiser."

"I said no. We wait."

The man who wanted to kill them pulled his hand behind his back, like he was reaching for something. She'd seen the thieves keep their guns in their waistbands when they'd arrived at the Fosters' place. Ellen thought she might be sick. "There's a lot of money at stake, and more. I hope you know what you're doing," he said.

"And I hope you don't even think about firing a weapon in here," said the man closest to them. He stepped between them and the angry thief. "Or there won't *be* any more money. For any of us. Boss has never steered us wrong before. This hasn't gone south, despite…" He glanced back at Ellen. Her breath caught in her throat at the malice in his eyes. He seemed to be taking her presence at their crime scene personally. As if he was angry at *her* for Rod's death. Did these men know him? Had Rod been a friend to some of them, too? "Not yet, anyway. I'll lock them in the walk-in until we're done here and boss tells us what to do with them. You, stand guard while they're inside."

One of the other men came with them as the first man led Ellen and Leo to the master bedroom's walk-in closet. The closet was huge and had an exposed lightbulb overhead, illuminating racks of summery clothing on either side. She swallowed hard on a burst of hope as they were shoved inside. The door's lock clicked behind them. She knew this house. She knew this room. And she knew this closet.

She glanced at Leo, but he kept his eyes downcast. Was he *praying*?

"Leo," she whispered. "Hey, listen."

He looked at her and shook his head, pointing to the door. They'd left the one man behind to guard them, and Leo had a point. They needed to be as quiet as possible with their plans. She nodded and backed up, heading toward the far rear of the walk-in closet. Leo furrowed his brow, asking her a silent question.

She reached down and slid aside several hangers that were laden with thick plaid shirts and warm jackets—always a necessity in northern BC, even during the summer months—and sighed in relief at the sight of the shiny gold handle she'd thought would be there. A number of the cottages she cleaned had large walk-in closets that were connected to both the master bedroom and a bathroom, but she hadn't been certain whether this cottage was one of those. The rooms in the cottages all blurred together in her mind sometimes.

She'd never been more relieved to be right. Leo rushed over as she pressed the small button on the side to unlock the connection between the closet and the bathroom on the other side, then closed her fingers around the handle and turned. The door opened.

Leo grabbed her wrist and squeezed, and she understood the gratitude in the gesture. With silent steps, they crept into the empty bathroom. The door was closed but not locked. Ellen wondered if she should lock the bathroom door, but decided against it. The risk that someone might hear the click of the latch was too great, and she didn't want to give any of the men an excuse to check on them.

When she turned back to Leo, his muscles were straining under the effort of sliding open the window without making a sound. The panel gave a slight hiss with each shift on its tracks, but Ellen doubted it'd be heard beyond the room they stood in. Once Leo opened it all the way, the only barrier that remained between them and escape from the house was a bug screen.

And a two-story drop to the ground.

"We can tie the clothes together," he whispered. "Make a rope out of the heavier fabrics and anchor it around the toilet or sink pipes. Lower ourselves down. Shouldn't take too many shirts or pants to reach down there."

"It's a good idea." Ellen leaned over, trying to figure out where the drop would take them. "But I think this room is right above one of the living room windows. If anyone looks out while we're lowering ourselves down, we'll be seen immediately."

Leo nodded and tapped his fingers on his pant leg. "Then we don't drop. We lower ourselves like rock climbers. If you can wrap one leg in the makeshift rope, you can walk down the side of the house, extending a little bit at a time, controlling the descent. That way you can shift your path around the windows. Then someone will only see us if they're pressed up against the window and looking outside." He narrowed his eyes at her. "But it'll take a lot of arm strength. Are you up for it?"

She shrugged. "It's not like we have any other options. Let's do it."

Leo kept a close eye on Ellen as they slipped clothing off the hangers and tied shirt arms and pant legs together. He found it baffling that folks were able to afford to keep reams of clothes at their vacation cottage—not to mention all the expensive artwork and modern appliances—but he took no issue with hardworking individuals affording themselves some luxuries, especially when their investments provided employment to locals like Ellen. God's blessings came in many forms, and it was what a person did with those blessings to help others that truly mattered.

She worked diligently alongside him, both of them cringing every time one of the hangers shifted and caused the tinny clang of metal on metal. Part of Leo hoped that the damage done to his phone was superficial, that maybe it still worked and was broadcasting their location—but he knew he shouldn't count on it. Also, the phone had looked awful, beyond hope. Which meant that they needed to get themselves out of there as fast as possible. If the RCMP showed up, it would be a nice bonus, but not something he was willing to place any stock in.

After about ten minutes, they'd created an enormous length of clothing rope that sat coiled in the center of the bathroom floor. Leo wrapped one end around the base of the toilet, knotting it and pulling it tight with all his strength. The makeshift rope would have to support both of their body weights without unraveling or tearing. He was more worried about the latter.

"I'll go first," he murmured to Ellen. "That way I can be at the bottom to catch you if the rope tears on your descent. You can watch me travel down and then do what I do."

The muscles in her throat shifted as she swallowed. Her nerves were showing, but she'd need to tamp them down again if they were going to make it out of the situation alive. Whoever the thieves' "boss" was, that person had clearly been the one calling the shots—literally—and Leo had no doubt that as soon as the thieves received their next instructions, it'd be the end of the line for himself and Ellen.

"You want *me* to be the one to fall?" She frowned. "I mean, our knots feel secure, but…"

"I'll catch you if it comes undone. I promise. But if you go first and I fall after you, there's no way I'm expecting you to catch me. And if I go down first and the rope breaks as I go, I'll probably be okay. If needed, you can jump from the window for me to catch you."

"Jump. From the window."

"Like I said, I promise to catch you."

She glanced sharply at the window and backed up until her knees bumped against the edge of the tub. "I don't think I can do this."

That was a new development. He hadn't heard her give any voice to weakness so far, despite Jamie's perception of his sister. "Of course you can. You drove a boat at nearly two hundred kilometers an hour on that lake and then pulled a James Bond move to evade our pursuers. You can certainly climb down the side of a house or jump from a window."

She shook her head, more rapidly this time. "You don't understand. I'm afraid of heights."

Of course she was. He'd known that while

they were kids, but it hadn't even occurred to him since they'd been reunited. And why would it? "Ellen, I don't want to push you or freak you out even more, but this is a matter of life or death. And I promise, I *promise* you, I'll be there to catch you if anything happens. Let me be your landing pad, your cushion. Unless you have a better option, this is our only exit and we're running out of time."

Footsteps sounded in the hall outside the bathroom. Leo's shoulders tensed. If they were discovered missing in the next few seconds, they'd be back to square one. Or dead. Ellen closed her eyes, squeezing hard. He wanted so much to wrap his arms around her and tell her that it was going to be okay, but even he was having trouble believing that the Lord would see them through this. If their survival wasn't in God's will, then he'd have to accept that. But God had also given him and Ellen brains and wits to use to the best of their abilities, which meant they had a responsibility to fight for life. Not to sit back and let evil win.

"Ellen?"

"Go," she whispered, eyes still closed. The footsteps in the hallway came closer and paused. "I'll watch and follow, I promise. Let's go."

He didn't waste a second. Leo dug his fingers into the edges of the window screen and yanked it out, praying with each breath that the men in the hallway wouldn't hear what they were doing or open the closet to check on them—or end their lives—in the next few minutes.

Raised voices, muffled but ardent, came from outside the room. Leo wrapped a section of the rope between his legs front to back, then around his leg from behind and up across the front of his chest. He draped the end over his shoulder and across his back so that he was holding the loose end of the rope with the arm opposite of the shoulder that the rope was draped over. After making sure that Ellen understood how to match the rope positioning for her own descent, he climbed up onto the window ledge, turned backward, tightened his grip and stepped off.

The strain on his wrists and fingers was immediate and painful, and he had a feeling that it would take longer than he'd like to get to the ground. Ellen's face appeared at the window, looking out as he lowered himself bit by bit. Her complexion was so pale and green that he thought she might pass out just watching his descent. He fervently hoped that she'd find the strength to step off the ledge after him.

He kept his eyes on her as he walked down the side of the house, shifting to a diagonal route to avoid the windows below—though it didn't take long to realize that it was going to be very difficult to prevent the rope from ever slipping sideways. There was a real possibility that only one of them might get to the ground before the men inside saw the rope and came running out after them.

Ellen looked over her shoulder, back at the bathroom door, then back at him. Worry filled her eyes. Had someone knocked on the door? She gestured at him to hurry. He increased his pace as much as he could safely manage, the pressure from the makeshift rope leaving burns as the fabric dug in and slid against his skin. When he bypassed the top edge of the living room window, he loosened his grip and dropped the final few meters. Then he released the rope so Ellen could pull it back up.

He held his breath as she disappeared from sight. Would she remember how to loop the rope around herself? When she poked her head out again, he gave her a thumbs-up, which she returned before climbing up onto the ledge. He positioned himself below her as she turned around and began the tentative process of supporting her own body weight.

During his descent, he hadn't felt the rope shift at all, so he had a feeling the biggest issue would be whether Ellen could hold herself up long enough to make it to the ground. But as she stepped off, feet planted on the side of the building, he couldn't help but note the muscles along her arms. She'd engaged her muscles from shoulders to forearms, and her biceps looked firm and strong. Cleaning houses was more physically demanding than he'd expected, clearly.

He wanted to call up to her to offer encouragement, but it wasn't worth the risk. As she reached the halfway mark, she turned her head and looked down at him. She saw the distance between herself and the ground, and a flash of panic crossed her features, disengaging her tight hold on the rope.

She gasped, a tiny shriek escaping as she slid down several feet before her grip tightened and she stabilized, body bouncing with the give of the fabric rope. Leo heard a tearing sound and lowered his stance as she shut her eyes and froze in place.

"Ellen," he whispered. "It's okay. You can let go now. You're far enough down that it won't be a long drop." She nodded, eyes still shut, but she didn't move.

A door slammed somewhere inside the house.

Ellen's eyes flew open and she looked down at him in fright. Had that been the bathroom door? It didn't matter—they didn't have time to stand around and contemplate whether or not their absence had been discovered.

She pressed her lips together, inhaled… and let go.

ELEVEN

It felt like her stomach had been left behind as she fell. Intellectually, she knew the drop wasn't far, but she couldn't help the rush of terror caused by the sensation of free-falling through the air. Almost instantly, the fear was abated as strong arms cradled her back and legs, stopping her momentum and keeping her from becoming a splat on the ground.

"I did it," she murmured. "I can't believe I did it."

"I can," Leo said. His voice brought sudden awareness to her arms, legs and torso. Her skin began to warm at the sensation of being held in his protective embrace—such an innocent gesture, and yet she couldn't stop her traitorous heart from beating a little faster.

Leo looked down at her with something akin to pride, and her stomach came back to her, this time twisting with anticipation. He lowered his face toward hers and she held her breath. Was he going to…kiss her?

And if he was, why wasn't she stopping it?

Because this is what I want, she admitted. Denying it wasn't going to work, not after this. Her limbs were just as frozen as they'd been before stepping off the ledge above, and her insides were entwined in the same knots. Fear mingled with surprise, but she welcomed it and closed her eyes—

And felt his lips plant on her forehead in a gentle, feathery kiss. The same kind of kiss a person gave their baby sister. Or their cat.

Disappointment coursed through her adrenaline-fueled limbs, sweeping aside the tension to shove a pile of exhaustion in its place.

"I'm proud of you," he said.

That only made it worse. But what could she say? This was neither the time nor the place to confront her emotions. "What do we do next? Which way?"

"The horses are just past this side of the wall, so we should—"

Another door slammed. Raised, angry voices sounded from inside, followed by more thumps. Closer this time.

"We need to get out of here," Leo said. He set her down and grabbed her hand, and despite her frustration, she didn't disagree with the urgency to get moving. They crept along the wall toward the backyard, but when they reached its edge, Leo jerked back and pressed his spine to the siding. He raised a finger to his lips.

The back door slid open and Ellen listened as men stepped outside, yelling at each other.

"Then search the perimeter! I don't care how long it takes, we can't let them escape this time. This operation is in enough hot water as it is."

"But we've already got what we came for, can't we just leave? We'll get them another time. They don't know who we are and haven't managed to track us down so far. I don't get why we keep going after them. We simply lie low, they don't find us and we're home free."

"You know that's not how boss wants to play this. Now that the RCMP have made a connection, it's only a matter of time before we get busted. We have to get in and out and eliminate obstacles along the way until we've—" The man stopped talking. "Did you hear that?"

Ellen looked at Leo, who shrugged. She hadn't heard anything, either. Leo peered around the corner, then flattened again, shaking his head.

Moments later, she heard the sound of car tires crunching against pavement.

"Could it be the ringleader?" she hissed. "Leo, if that's their boss—"

He nodded, then looked around the corner again. "They're gone. If that's the boss of this band of thieves, they might have a meeting. They'll be distracted. Actually…" He raised one eyebrow. "How do you feel about jacking a car?"

"Do you know how to do that? And how are we going to get to the front of the house without anyone seeing?"

He didn't answer, but lowered himself all the way to the ground and began crawling forward on his belly.

Before she'd witnessed Rod's death and the robbery, Ellen had loved the open-concept layout of the lake's vacation cottages—the giant windows all around the main living area, letting the light in and warming each building naturally. The sunlight had always been comforting, soothing. A wonderful change from the days when she'd cleaned local office buildings and retail stores. She still took those contracts sometimes to supplement her work at Schroeder Lake, but those places tended to be dark, a little dingy and a bit depressing at times due to the lack of natural light and the proliferation of fluorescent bulbs.

She flopped down, too. The cool grass felt oddly refreshing on the fabric burns across her hands. When Leo moved, she saw the matching burns on his hands, though his looked much angrier. They belly-crawled across the side of the house toward the front. She held her breath as they passed beneath the windows. Raised voices still came from inside, but no one ran toward them waving a gun, which was a comforting thing.

As they approached the edge of the exterior, an electronic whoop filled the air. Leo froze and Ellen paused behind him. He looked back at her, puzzled. Then he leaped to his feet and ran toward the front of the house.

Alarmed, she did the same, though she couldn't help but wonder whether the events of the day had taken a sudden toll on him, if he'd maybe taken a blow to the head that she hadn't seen—but as she rounded the corner of the house, she saw why he'd run.

An RCMP patrol car sat in the driveway. The car doors swung open, and Staff Sergeant Clyne slid out of the driver's seat while Trucco climbed out of the passenger side.

Less than a second passed before yet another RCMP vehicle rolled into the driveway. Her brother sat behind the wheel.

"Clyne!" Leo shouted as he ran toward the officer. "Trucco, get back in the car! There are armed men inside!"

The staff sergeant's attention snapped from Leo's approach to the forensic examiner, who'd exited the car. "Get back in the vehicle, Ms. Trucco, before you get yourself killed!"

As Jamie rushed from his patrol car to the staff sergeant's side, the front door to the cottage opened.

Leo stilled his steps and Ellen almost bumped into him from the unexpected halt. All movement slowed, as if every person in the vicinity was moving through syrup. One of the thieves stood in the doorway, his weapon raised. Fear seared across Ellen's brain as both her brother and Clyne simultaneously reached for their sidepieces.

Jamie, farthest from cover, was right in the line of fire and she didn't know what to do.

"Let's go, Biers!" Clyne shouted, and the world spun into motion again. Instead of firing, the thief in the doorway bolted without another moment's hesitation.

"Go, go, go!" shouted men inside the house.

She heard thumps and scrambling as her brother followed the detachment leader, and her gut churned with anxiety for Jamie's safety.

"This way, Ellen." Leo motioned her toward Jamie's patrol car. A horse trailer was attached to the back of the vehicle. "We're vulnerable out here if there's an exchange of fire. We need to be able to move if the scene gets hot."

She allowed herself to be led behind the trailer. They crouched, waiting. Leo's arm draped across her shoulders and she found herself involuntarily leaning into him. She straightened, cheeks on fire.

"Sorry," she mumbled.

He offered a questioning glance. "For what?"

"I didn't mean to… Never mind." Of course he didn't get it—he didn't feel the same way as she had to admit she did. She was falling fast, in a real way, for this man, in a way that transcended childhood sentiment, while he felt for her how a person did for a small, helpless puppy.

That wasn't fair. He'd never called her helpless, and so far he'd respected all her requests to treat her normally and not with kid gloves like Jamie often did. Leo hadn't offered platitudes or condescending remarks when her doubts about God came up, and never once had he given false encouragement in a moment where he wasn't certain himself about the outcome.

But he didn't see her the way she'd begun to see him. All of those things had burrowed into her heart and given her a new perspective on the middle Thrace brother. He was strong and confident—as well as handsome—and ultimately considerate toward her point of view in a way that other men she'd tried to date had never been. Plus, he was able to handle Jamie without being intimidated, also unlike the other men she'd tried to date. Yes, she'd had plenty of conversations with her brother regarding how much influence he had over her life, but at the end of the day, she was glad he cared. And she knew that if she ever fell in love, he wouldn't stand in her way.

Unless that person was an RCMP officer himself, in which case, she had a feeling that her relationship with Jamie would become very, very strained.

Not that I'll ever have to worry about that. She glanced over and caught Leo watching her. When his tiny smile caused her heart to skip a beat, she knew she was in trouble— from more than thieves and bullets.

Though she had a feeling she'd rather face

those than her brother if he ever found out how she felt about Leo Thrace.

It had taken every ounce of his self-control not to kiss Ellen when she'd dropped into his arms. She'd fit there so perfectly, her light but muscular body an easy burden—indeed, not a burden at all—and he'd had a rather vivid vision of holding her this way as he stepped across the threshold of his home. *Their* home.

He'd dropped to his belly to crawl across the grass without giving Ellen much warning, because he'd needed to separate himself from her before he did something stupid. The grass rubbing against the burns on his palms and the earth digging into his joints had quickly replaced the memory of her curves, the soft skin of her forehead under his lips. The strange look in her eyes when he'd pulled away had questioned what on earth he was doing.

Truth be told, he didn't know. He couldn't explain the emotions that had quickly built up during the hours in her presence, stacking layer upon layer until he felt he might explode if he didn't tell her how he felt. But that look in her eyes when he'd drawn back had been enough—it told him exactly how *she* felt about being close to him, and boy, had it hurt.

Why he'd draped his arm over her shoulders as they hid behind the horse trailer, waiting for his best friend and the staff sergeant, he had no idea. Glutton for punishment? Perhaps. He wished he had his gear so he could run inside and help the other men, but then again, staying by Ellen's side was just as important a job. At any moment, one of the thieves could rush outside the house with the bright idea of taking a hostage, or—

The front door opened, and Ellen's gasp was sharp beside him. A weary-looking staff sergeant and his fellow officer emerged with a third man between them.

"They caught one of the thieves!" Ellen's lips parted, and Leo swallowed hard at the sight. He needed to push past distraction and think about this huge break in the case instead.

He turned back to the approaching crew. "This is fantastic. Between this guy and Hogan, maybe we can start getting some answers."

"Did you hear any shots? I didn't hear any gunfire."

"I don't think there was an exchange of shots. With two uniformed RCMP officers arriving on-scene, the thieves would have to be incredibly stupid to start a gun battle. And we don't even know if those are real guns or the rubber bullet dupes, so an exchange of fire with police could have been suicide."

He'd been thinking all this time that the men were crazy to fire at Ellen *and* him, considering his death would spur a deep federal investigation with swarms of officers and specialists scouring the area for the thieves, but that was thinking like an officer of the law. The thieves had seemed to know he was in law enforcement, but how would they have any idea that he was RCMP? He'd been wearing plain clothes this whole time and ever since he'd arrived in the area, so of course the thieves wouldn't know.

"Clear!" Jamie called.

Leo tapped Ellen's shoulder and stood. He wanted to blurt out so many questions, but this wasn't his case and he didn't want to upset the staff sergeant again. He'd stepped on the man's toes enough.

Fortunately, Jamie knew his friend well. "The guys scattered as soon as they saw us coming. This character was farthest away from the crew, though, so we were able to catch him. Isn't that right, Nick?"

"You know this guy?" Leo couldn't help it. That was a big deal.

The staff sergeant huffed a laugh. "Know

him? He's only the most notorious carjacker in the area. Mind you, that's not saying much, but at least it's an accomplishment he can brag to his buddies about. Isn't that right, Nick?" Clyne opened the door of Jamie's car for the perp and waited while he climbed inside. "And remember that you have the right to keep quiet. I suggest you do." He shut the door and sighed. "It's not much, but it could be something. Hope so, since that old man isn't talking. It was a fantastic lead you gave us, though. I apologize for shouting at you this morning, Ms. Biers, Officer Thrace, but I hope you understand why."

Clyne extended his hand and Leo took it for a firm handshake. "No harm done," Leo said, grateful for the assist.

Ms. Trucco slid out of the front seat again, her perpetual scowl unchanged except for a touch of worry that creased her brow. "Can we please move along now?"

"Old Hogan," Jamie said, ignoring the woman's protest and glancing at Leo. "Guy's laced up tighter than a goalie's shin pads. Won't look at anyone, won't talk to us except to say he doesn't know anything. I've told him that we might have to press charges for obstruction, but he won't budge."

"Sounds like he's scared." Ellen's voice

shook. She seemed to be fighting to keep it steady. "Hogan's not known for his jauntiness, but he's not a bad person. So far as I know, anyway. He's always been pleasant and respectful, if a little gruff. I figure he's just old and ornery. If he's not talking, he's worried about something. Otherwise he'd tell you he doesn't know anything and go back to work. He loves his job."

"That's what it seems like to me, too," Jamie said. "But either way, we're not going to get far until one of these two speaks up. Hopefully this guy will roll on his crew, because he's not going to do himself any favors by keeping silent. Especially when there's a homicide investigation at play."

Leo looked over at Ellen. He didn't miss how the dark circles under her eyes had deepened further. The color in her cheeks still hadn't returned. She needed to rest. "Obviously we still need to head to the station and give our reports, but before we get moving—how did you two know where to find us? I was on a call with Jamie when we were run down on the main road, but my phone got run over."

Jamie looked at the staff sergeant and back at Leo. "Believe it or not, your phone didn't die. It just got a little flattened, but the GPS kept working. I had one of the guys hitch up the horse trailer in case one of the horses had been injured, and then headed for your location on the map. If we hadn't set up the phone-finder app yesterday, who knows how long we'd have been searching for you."

"I wondered if that might be the case." An immense wave of gratitude washed over Leo for God's provision. "Between the community center and where we were almost run off the road, the thieves must have approximated where we'd end up. They sent some men after us so we couldn't mess up their next job, I guess. That's what I gathered from their conversation. We've been trying to outrun them all day, and they finally got the upper hand and caught up."

"Well, they certainly don't have the upper hand anymore. That said, if Clyne hadn't left for the community center seconds after Aaron's call about what happened on the lake, I'm less confident things would have gone down as smoothly as they did just now." Jamie looked over his shoulder at the forensic examiner.

Since Trucco seemed uninterested in entering the conversation, Clyne clarified, "I was taking Trucco out to do some preliminary forensics based on what Aaron mentioned about the bullets. She's got another day here, so might as well use the resources we have. I was glad to hear the injuries were minor. Could have been much worse, even with rubber bullets."

"Fully agreed, sir." Leo ran his hand through his hair, feeling suddenly exhausted. "I assume at least one of these cars is heading back to the station? The horses aren't hurt, but they're probably tired after all we've put them through today, so they might appreciate a ride. As would we. The trails are too muddy and I'm not keen on getting run over again."

"Me, either," Ellen said. "Do you need help loading the horses?"

"Please." Jamie walked around the back of the trailer and opened the doors. "Show me where they are?"

Leo felt a twinge in his heart as she walked away with her brother. Since the staff sergeant had his back to the house, the man missed the moment when Jamie—likely sensing a show of emotion wouldn't be noticed by his superior—bear-hugged his little sister. Ellen pushed away from him and swatted his arm, so Jamie hugged her again. Their playful engagement continued until they were out of sight at the back of the house. A sense of loss began to envelop Leo. He'd been able to banter playfully with Ellen, too, when they were younger, but hugs and nudges meant different things now. His heart had betrayed him by falling hard and fast for someone who needed to stay just a friend.

"You two might as well come with me," said Clyne, breaking through Leo's self-reflection. "Biers will head back to the station with the suspect and the horses. There's more room in my vehicle, less risk. Trucco can go with him, too."

"Appreciate that, sir." Leo sighed, ignoring the sputter of protest from Trucco, who'd undoubtedly heard Clyne's comment. "And I appreciate you taking the time to personally assist on this case. I know how short-staffed rural detachments are, and you must have a lot on your plate right now."

"That I do." The man planted his hands on his hips. "But Rod Kroeker was a well-loved figure in this community. The thieves might have been able to continue their work without detection—or at least, much interference beyond what we already knew—if they hadn't caused a man's death. Accident or not, the town wants justice. It's almost a relief to be out here rather than stuck in my office fielding call after call. The front desk has had two hundred and twelve calls come in since that local reporter blabbed on the news. Can you believe it?"

"Yes, sir. Unfortunately, I *can* believe it."

"What I can't believe," Ms. Trucco interrupted, "is that neither of you are going to take me to the community center? Everyone is fine, no one got hurt, but if this case isn't solved quickly, the way I see it? Another death is inevitable."

Clyne's jaw tightened, and Leo sympathized with the man. Trucco likely didn't even realize how abrasive she sounded, but Leo didn't begrudge her tone. He suspected she had to fight hard to be taken seriously in her field, and she made a good point. Getting the forensics taken care of quickly could help save a life, and the longer this situation dragged on, the more the thieves' desperation seemed to escalate. He could only pray that they took the thieves down before they killed someone else, regardless of accident or intention.

"Why doesn't Trucco come with us, anyway," Leo suggested. "We're not far from the community center, and it's unwise to have her ride with Jamie and the suspect. We can drop her off at the community center. Aaron and Sam can assist her in any way she needs, then you can take Ellen and me back to the station."

The staff sergeant raised an eyebrow. "You're sure they'd help? I was going to observe her work for learning purposes, but if your brothers are willing to lend a hand, that's the more practical course of action."

"Consider it done. I'll give them a call now." Leo nodded at Trucco to acknowledge the matter was settled, and her features softened. "Can I borrow someone's phone?"

"Thank you," she said. "Here, use mine." She handed off her cell, then slid back into the passenger seat of Clyne's car.

By the time Leo finished his call to his brothers, Ellen and Jamie had rounded the corner of the cottage, each leading a horse. The animals were moving slowly, and Leo was glad for his friend's quick thinking to bring along the trailer.

After the horses were loaded up and the suspect secured in Jamie's vehicle, Leo and Ellen climbed into the back seat of the staff sergeant's patrol car as Jamie pulled away.

It didn't take long for Clyne to reach the community center. He and Trucco exited the vehicle to talk to Aaron and Sam, though Leo chose to stay inside the car with Ellen. As much as he wanted to get out and help, the thieves were still out there—and they could be anywhere. Ellen also had grown very still and quiet, and he didn't like the idea of leaving her alone.

Once they were back on the road, minus one forensic examiner, Clyne turned down the police radio.

"You two need anything? Food, coffee? We've got a few things at the station, but I know it's been a long day for you."

"That's very kind," Ellen said. "But I don't want to take up any more of your time. We can order in, or I'll have a friend bring something over to us. Is that okay with you?" She looked at Leo, but his hunger evaporated as she regarded him with her crystalline blue eyes.

"I'm… Yeah, that's fine. Whatever you like, I can work with."

She tilted her head, a tiny but curious smile touching her lips. "If you're sure."

The staff sergeant cleared his throat. "Uh, well…that's all well and good, but I have another suggestion. And you might not like it."

"Oh?" Leo straightened his spine at the serious tone in the man's voice. "And what's that?"

"It's my professional recommendation that you don't return to the station. I didn't want to mention it while Trucco was still in here, because these criminals have proven they've got a line to you just about anywhere. They could be talking to anyone, extracting information in ways we haven't even thought of."

The statement increased Leo's weariness. "How so?"

Clyne sighed before continuing, sounding as frustrated as Leo felt. "Officer Biers mentioned that only officers inside the detachment knew that you were going to the community center, and yet the assailants found you there, anyway. That sounds like an inside job. I'm worried that if I bring you two back to the station after everything that's gone down today, whoever's behind this might decide they've had enough."

He cleared his throat, and Leo had a feeling he knew what was coming next. "If you go back to the station? There's a very real possibility that I'd be handing you over to the very person, or people, who want you dead."

TWELVE

Ellen hoped she'd heard the staff sergeant wrong. After all, the police station was supposed to be the safest place in the entire town. If they couldn't go there, where else could they go? Would he make them leave town entirely? She could get on a bus and head south to stay with some friends, but even that seemed like a risky proposition. These thieves had her name and knew what she looked like, so if they found her isolated while traveling to a place she wasn't all that familiar with—

"Hey, breathe." Leo's hand landed on her arm. She flinched at the touch but didn't pull away. "I see you panicking. We're going to get through this."

"No need to panic just yet," Clyne said, picking up on Leo's words. "In fact, I have a suggestion, and if you're up for it, it'll be between the three of us."

Ellen took a deep breath and stared out the

window at the trees whipping by. "I guess options are limited at this point, so go ahead."

"There's a motel up the road. It's east of the lake and a little north of town. It's where we put up visiting officers so that they can experience the sense of being in the isolated northern wilderness without being too far from the station. It's about a fifteen-minute trip between the motel and the station. Plus, and you didn't hear it from me, it's all our budget allows." He chuckled without humor. "But we work with this place all the time, so I know it's secure. And if we drive you over right now, it means that only the two of you and myself need to know that you're there. I'll check you in anonymously, get your rooms side by side. I'll even personally have someone send a pizza up and tell them to leave it outside the door so that nobody sees you're inside. How does that sound?"

It sounded pretty good, in fact, but Ellen did feel a little weird about not telling Jamie. "What about my brother? He'll panic if he doesn't know where I am."

Clyne grunted. "I understand. I have a younger sister. We can call him right now, if you want." He began punching buttons on the dashboard. "It needs to stay between the four of us, though."

"Yeah. Yes, please. But…if you call him on the radio, what if he's still in the car with the suspect? Or if someone else overhears on the radio?" Another wave of fear rushed through her. With how involved Jamie had become in this case, was *he* now in danger, too?

Clyne hesitated, then nodded. "Smart. Once I drop you off, I'll head directly back to the station and tell him in person."

"That seems like the wisest course of action at this point," Leo said. He squeezed her hand. "Though if you're not okay with this, we'll find another option."

Was she okay with it? Not entirely. She shut her eyes, trying to consider the situation without the distractions of everything and everyone around her. Jamie had work to do. He had a new suspect to question, and if that man talked, maybe Old Hogan would open up, too. He had a new crime scene to investigate—two of them, in fact—and having her around at the station might actually be a distraction to him. Knowing that she was safe and secure in a secret location, far from any possible prying eyes or danger, could help Jamie to focus and come to a resolution sooner.

In her mind, that settled it. "All right. Let's do it."

With her confirmation, the staff sergeant

turned the car around to head the opposite direction. Leo kept his hand connected with hers, which was both a comfort and a frustration, but she didn't pull away.

They drove the rest of the way in silence, though the staff sergeant turned up his radio to hear the updates from his team. The crackling sound of the traffic reports, case updates and general banter helped to calm her nerves and bring her breathing back down to a steady, calm rhythm, and with her adrenaline firing at normal levels, her arms finally felt the delayed-onset muscle soreness of rappelling down the side of a building. She was quite fit from all the cleaning work she did, but the climbing exercise had forced her to engage different muscles and use every ounce of physical strength she possessed.

The patrol car pulled off the highway and into a parking lot for the White Dogwood Motel. The faded blue siding with white window framing and off-white doors for each unit were reminiscent of decades past, but coloring aside, the exterior looked well kept and neat. The motel was one long building with the room units all in a row, with the check-in office located at the far end. The parking spaces lined the lot right in front of the rooms, facing the road. Clyne climbed out of the car and leaned over to speak to them.

"I'll go check you in. Won't be a minute. Two rooms, side by side?"

Leo nodded once, and the staff sergeant tapped the top of the car, then closed his door and headed inside.

"I'm ready for this to be over," Leo said. She looked over at him, fully aware that their hands remained connected. His thumb slid across the surface of her skin, sending sparks up her arm. "Which I realize is a massive understatement, but I'm even more ready now than I was a few hours ago. My shoulders and biceps are on *fire*."

He smiled wryly as he spoke, and she couldn't help laughing. "Mine, too. My hands don't look as bad as yours do, though. Those cloth burns still look painful. Maybe we should have asked the staff sergeant to stop for some salve."

Leo shrugged. "I'll be fine. There's usually a cheap moisturizer inside motel rooms, right? That'll do for tonight. I'm not too worried about it. I can endure a little extra pain if it means giving the officers the time and space they need to get a handle on what's been going on with this case."

"I really hope Old Hogan talks." She

sighed. "I'm sure that whatever he's gotten himself messed up in, it wasn't intentional. He probably knows exactly who he gave that cigarette to and is afraid to say it."

"That gives even greater weight to someone on the inside being behind this, though. If he knows who it is and it's someone at the station, I'm not surprised he's keeping his mouth shut. I might, too, in his situation. But let's not discount Trucco's findings, also. She may be a little rough around the edges, but there's a reason she's traveling around as a visiting instructor. It means she does good work and she's well respected. She could be the one to break open this case."

Ellen rubbed her forehead. A spark of pain shot up the back of her neck and into her skull. "I think I need to lie down. The events of the day are catching up to me."

Leo chuckled, but it was a gentle, understanding sound. "It's about time, Ellen. You're not superhuman." His hand slipped underneath hers, interlacing their fingers, and she found herself caught in his gaze. "Though, if I do say so, you're a pretty *super* human."

She couldn't help it. It was so cheesy that she laughed.

His shoulders sagged and he pulled his hand away, groaning. "Okay, okay. I deserved that." He smiled. "But I mean it, Ellen. I know we haven't seen each other all that much for the past number of years."

She blinked, and his face was closer to hers than she remembered it being moments before. She felt very aware of the dryness inside her mouth and the fact that she hadn't brushed her teeth since early that morning. Her arms felt like lead weights, and yet the muscles in her back propelled her forward, closer to Leo, closer to his parted lips and his heavily lidded eyes that had somehow, inexplicably and yet hopefully, landed on her mouth—

The car door swung open.

"All taken care of—oops, sorry. Am I interrupting?" Clyne poked his head in as he spoke, a knowing grin spreading across his face as she and Leo leaped away from each other like teenagers caught by their parents. "The rooms are at the far end. They're separate units but connected by a door that can be locked or unlocked from either side, 'family-style,' I think it's called. I'll drive us down so there's less risk of you being spotted. Here are the room keys."

He passed the keys back, one for each room, and chauffeured them to the far end of the motel.

"This is where I leave you," he said. "But

I'll send a little something over for you both, all right? I'll tell the delivery guy to knock and leave it outside. And when we've got a lead or when I think it's safe to come back to town, I'll either call the front desk and have them get a cab back for you, or myself or one of the others will come for you. I'll speak to Jamie as soon as I'm back at the station. Don't risk calling in. We have no clue who might pick up, and this place is only safe as long as no one knows you're here. All right?"

"Thank you, sir." Leo's words were stiff and formal, and he didn't turn his head toward her at all. Ellen's cheeks burned with embarrassment. Had she imagined what had happened between them before Clyne returned to the car? Was Leo upset with her?

"Yes, thank you," she squeaked. She opened the car door and reached her room in two strides, taking the end unit. She unlocked it and was about to step inside when Leo called her name.

"What?"

The easy smile he'd had minutes before was gone, replaced by a stern, professional demeanor. "I'll be right here if you need anything or if you want to talk. But I suggest we both get as much rest as possible."

She agreed. *As much rest as possible.*

And hopefully, resting would not only heal her bruised and aching body, but her sore and confused heart, as well.

Leo shut the door behind him, then leaned against it. He banged the back of his head against the door once, but immediately regretted the action. Just like he regretted what had almost happened in the patrol car. After everything they'd been through, after all the promises he'd made to himself less than an hour earlier, he'd gone ahead and nearly kissed her, anyway. What had he been thinking?

He *hadn't* been thinking. And that was the problem. Without a clear head and a direct sense of his responsibilities, how could he be the protector Ellen needed right now? She didn't need a guy making moves on her. It wasn't fair to her; she had enough on her plate.

And it wasn't fair to her brother to go behind his back after making a promise.

He slid over to the window, nudging aside the gauzy white curtain to check outside the room. The sun had descended considerably in the past few hours, sending its golden and orange rays overtop the tree line to craft a beautiful, picturesque view of the forest across the road. When he was younger, he'd taken the lush surroundings of northern British Columbia for granted, not truly appreciating its majesty until after he'd left the area for several years to attend college in Saskatchewan for his police foundations diploma. Graduation was followed by his RCMP training in other parts of the country. Each province had its own remarkable views and natural beauty, but his heart was partial to the place in which he was born and raised.

The parking lot outside the motel was empty, save for one little gray Civic that he suspected belonged to the owner. The near-complete vacancy wasn't a surprise; tourist season didn't begin for another few weeks. Most folks who moved through the area in need of lodging at this time of year were contractors and long-range truckers.

Still, he didn't feel right about falling asleep while the thieves remained at large and were still angry at Ellen and looking for a way to permanently silence her. Especially now that the RCMP had one of the thieves in custody. And if the police were able to round up a few more suspects, both she and now he would have a solid shot at identifying the rest of the thieves by voice if necessary. That was, if the suspect Clyne and Jamie had arrested didn't roll on the rest of his team first. But if there was any truth to the idea that there was a dirty cop in the detachment, that might not happen, either. The suspect might be just as freaked out as Hogan.

Leo pulled the second set of blinds closed about three quarters of the way, then took the padded metal chair from the motel room's desk and positioned it at the end of the window ledge. The way the blinds draped, if he sat at the edge of the window, he could see through the space between the glass and the fabric, but it'd be difficult for anyone outside to see him. From this angle, he could keep an eye on the front door of Ellen's room to see when the food arrived.

Or trouble. But he hoped the former would be their only visitor that night.

He sat there for what felt like hours. Night fully descended, until the only illumination outside came from the stars and moon overhead, and the dim, flickering bulb inside the motel sign. The stars sparkling in the sky offered a surreal contrast to the madness of the past day and a half.

Leo didn't hear a peep from Ellen's room, though more than once he got up to put his ear against the interior door that connected the two units.

Has it really only been a day and a half, Lord? Leo ran his hands down his face, stopping halfway to rub his eyes. *How can I feel this strongly for her after such a short time?*

But he knew very well how. He'd known her for a lot longer than a day and a half, and his heart had never truly given up its affections—rather, he'd shoved all those emotions aside for the sake of his friendship and for Ellen.

But the tragedy that had befallen Ellen's mother and had possibly traumatized her had happened a long time ago, though. They were older now. Wiser and better equipped to tackle what life threw at them, and if the past day and a half had taught him anything, it was that the meek, adorable Ellen he'd grown up knowing had blossomed into a courageous, breathtaking version of herself.

His eyelids began to droop and his stomach gnawed on itself. *Where is that pizza?*

He had decided to get up and grab some water to help keep awake when a knock came on the door between the rooms.

When he unlocked it, Ellen stood on the other side, bleary-eyed and crestfallen.

"I can't sleep," she said. She glanced up at him and sighed, shaking her head. "I'm sorry.

I don't know why I came in here. I'll leave you alone." She turned to leave.

"No, Ellen!" He reached for her and lightly brushed her wrist. She paused, gazing back at him with sorrowful—no, teary—eyes. "Oh, Ellie."

She broke. She plowed headfirst into his chest, rivers of tears flooding her cheeks and soaking his shirt. He wrapped his arms around her as tightly as he could and held her there. Her shoulders shook with the force of emotion, and he searched for the right words to help her feel better—but at the same time, he knew that words would never be enough to relieve the grief, the agony and the trauma that had begun the moment those thieves walked into the house where she worked.

In fact, it relieved *him* a little to see her release everything she'd been holding back. He'd started to worry whether it might all catch up with her at the wrong time or when she least expected it. Here in his arms, she could be vulnerable. He saw the strength in her weakness and felt honored that she trusted him enough to show this side of herself to him.

When her sobs began to abate, he took her by the shoulders and led her to the edge of the bed. He sat her down, retrieved the box of

Kleenex from the bathroom and then took a seat in the metal chair across from her.

"Take as long as you need," he said, though what he really wanted to do was hold her again. His arms felt empty and cold without her in them.

After several minutes, she wrapped her arms around her stomach and blinked up at him. "Leo, why is this happening? Haven't I suffered enough?"

He wanted to tell her why, but he didn't have an answer. And he wanted to offer reassurance for her pain, but she didn't want to hear it—she'd made that quite clear.

"Did you get any rest?" he asked instead, since it seemed like the safer thing to say and because he genuinely cared whether she'd had a chance to recover. "There hasn't been any food delivered yet, but I'm sure it's for a good reason. Something might have come up that has kept Clyne from making a call. Or he just plumb forgot. Either way, there's still motel tea and coffee. And we can always drink those little creamer cups or eat the sugar packets if need be."

Her nose wrinkled. "That sounds awful."

"Worse than having a sour stomach all night?"

"Too late." She sighed and tucked her knees

up to her chin. "But to answer your question, no. I didn't get any rest. I can't sleep. I keep seeing… Never mind." She turned away from him, resting her cheek on her knees and curling her arm around her face.

"Ellen." He slipped from the metal chair into the space next to her. "It's all right. We've known each other a long time, and you have to know that I'll help you however I can."

"It's stupid," she mumbled into her arm. "I'm a grown woman."

"It's not stupid. And it doesn't matter how old or how young you are. The things that happen in life, especially difficult or traumatic things, can affect you in various ways at any point. You went through the loss of both of your parents at a young age, so that's bound to shape the way you see and relate to the world."

She took a shaky breath and raised her head, switching to the other cheek so he could see her. "Did Jamie ever tell you that I was in the house when my mom died? In the next room? She was making me a snack. I should have made it myself, but she wanted to do it, even though she'd already taken all those pills. Not that I knew she'd taken them. It was like…like she wanted to do one last thing for me to say goodbye. At the time I thought she'd maybe gotten better because she was in such a good mood and I hadn't seen her like that for months. Since Dad died, really. How stupid was I to think that?"

His heart broke for her and he searched for the right words. "You were a teenager. How could you have known? And if she'd taken the pills already, there wasn't anything you could have done. By the time an ambulance arrived—"

"You think I don't know that?" She sat upright, knees dropping. Color blazed across her skin. "I've replayed that day over and over a thousand times. It comes to me when I least expect it. I'll hear a sound, or see a color, or smell a particular scent... Look, if I'd been in the kitchen with her, she might not have fallen. The doctors said the head injury from the fall, combined with what was already in her system, was what killed her. Her body wasn't able to fight or recover." She took a shaky inhale. "And then seeing Rod fall... hearing him hit the ground..."

Leo understood now. It was like she'd pulled back a curtain that he hadn't even known had been there all this time, but that clarified all of Jamie's comments and concerns about Ellen's mental health and wellbeing. He gently took her hand and she didn't pull away. "Ellen, I'm going to ask you a question and I don't want you to think I'm being patronizing, because I really don't know if anyone has suggested this to you. Sometimes these types of things get overlooked or shoved aside, or we don't have anyone in our lives with the experience to identify what might be wrong. But…has anyone talked to you about post-traumatic stress disorder?"

THIRTEEN

She looked taken aback, and pulled her hand away as if his touch burned her. "I don't have PTSD, Leo. I think I'd know."

"Has your doctor talked to you about it? Have you told anyone about these moments when the memories come back to you?"

She swallowed, her throat moving delicately. She took a long pause before responding, and when she did, her voice was quiet. "No."

"These things you're describing, these flashes of memory that come to you—triggered by a sound or a smell or a specific visual cue—it's a classic example of PTSD."

"But I'm not a soldier or a foreign aid worker." She laughed bitterly. "I'm just a woman who cleans houses for rich people."

He shook his head and took her hands again. "You're not 'just' anything, Ellen. And it's not only soldiers who have PTSD. Anyone who has experienced severe trauma of any kind can develop it, and it's nothing to be ashamed of. There's treatment and support, and there are tried-and-true coping mechanisms that can help so that you don't go through life wondering when the next attack is going to hit."

He thought back to the time they'd spent together these past couple of days. There'd been moments when she'd seemed to space out, to go someplace else in her mind—and other times when she'd almost mechanically pushed forward, robotic and cold. "Have you had these moments during our time together? Like when you needed to be alone in the diner washroom?"

She nodded, but didn't speak. Her shoulders began to creep toward her ears, full of tension.

He squeezed her hands. "It's all right. We're going to get through this and get you the help you need to get better, or at least learn how to cope in a way that has a lesser effect on your quality of life." A suggestion sprang to mind but he tried to shove it aside, certain that she'd be upset with him for bringing it up. "I know you probably don't want to hear about solutions right now, not when there's something bigger to worry about, but trust me when I say that it will make a difference. If you try to go back to work after this—especially to the Fosters' to clean—I'm worried that you'll be triggered when no one is around to help bring you back down."

Her next inhale was shaky and uncertain. "I'm going to end up like my mother, aren't I?" It wasn't a question but a statement. As if she'd thought a lot about it.

"What? Of course not. What makes you say that?"

She met his gaze. "I can't handle reality. You want to put me on pills. I can see where this is going."

"You're not your mother. You control your life. You make the decisions, medical or otherwise, and you have a brother who's looking out for you. He'd love to help you in any way he can, I'm sure of it."

Her face fell at the mention of Jamie, and the tears began to flow a second time. "Leo… will you… I can't believe I'm saying this. But will you pray for me?"

Guilt sliced through Leo's insides. He'd felt the urge to pray for her but had been afraid she'd get angry at him—but when God had a plan, He made it happen regardless of human fallacy. *Forgive me, Lord.* "Of course I will."

"And will you—" she inhaled through

her tears, the wetness causing her to cough "—ask why He abandoned us?"

Leo felt taken aback. "Abandoned you? God hasn't abandoned you, Ellen."

"Yes, He has. He took my dad away. I begged Him not to take away my mom and it happened, anyway. I asked God every single day to help my mom get better, but she only got worse. God doesn't care. I went to church from a baby until eighteen, as faithful as anyone, but it wasn't enough. He lets terrible things happen to good people, and then He throws them away like garbage. I didn't matter enough, and my family didn't matter enough. My mom didn't matter enough."

"Ellen, bad things happen to good people because we live in a broken world. Look around. All you have to do is read the news on any given morning to see how messed up things are, but it's not that God doesn't care. It's that He gave humanity free will, and that means the choice to turn the world into a trash fire as much as it does to do good. On a more personal level, we don't always know why bad things happen. It's hard to understand, especially in the depths of pain. But I do believe that God can use bad things for good. He can make beauty out of tragedy, though we can't always see, understand or be ready to accept that when we're in the midst of the situation."

She sniffed. "I feel like I've been in the midst of the situation for a solid fifteen years. Almost twenty, if you count losing my father."

Leo shifted closer to her. "I'll pray for you now, if you like." She nodded and closed her eyes, and Leo followed suit. He offered up a brief but sincere prayer that touched on her concerns, but also asked for safety and protection in their current crisis. He opened his eyes after speaking "amen" to find Ellen's tears pouring down her face again. He held up the box of tissues, but it was empty. "Uh-oh. All out. Should I grab a towel from the bathroom?"

Ellen nodded, but didn't speak—and that was when he noticed the pace of her breathing had sped up and her eyes had gone slightly unfocused. Sweat broke out along her forehead.

"Ellen?"

She didn't respond and instead hunched over like she'd lost control of her core muscles.

Leo could have kicked himself. In the process of speaking about PTSD triggers, they'd gone ahead and triggered an attack—he should have known better.

He scooped her up without another moment's hesitation and carried her into the washroom, then set her down on the wide lip of the bathtub. He pulled down a towel, mopped the sweat off her brow and then poured cold water over a washcloth. He wrung it out and pressed it against her forehead. She swayed where she sat, and he thought back to his RCMP crisis training. Firm pressure on the body, much like a thunder shirt for anxious dogs, worked on humans, too, to bring down the cortisol levels and stop the adrenal glands from releasing constant waves of stress hormones.

He sat beside her and pulled her into his arms. His right arm reached around her back to keep the cold compress on her forehead.

When her breathing sped up, he held her tighter. When she began to tilt sideways, he raised her head. And when she finally came back to him with a new wave of tears, he pressed his cheek against her in gratitude for God's mercy, his own unbidden flood mixing with hers.

Finally, she released a shaky, shuddering breath, and turned her head to look at him.

He searched her face, seeking a sign of

another attack, hoping that whatever he said next would be healing and not harmful. He should have known better than to engage her in talk about the past while they were still dealing with the danger of the present. He should have realized that what she needed from him was friendship and nothing more. He should have—

"Leo?" She spoke in a hushed whisper, lips parting.

He found that he could barely speak. "Yes?"

"This might be the wrong time for this, but… I don't know what's going to happen next. I don't know if we'll make it out of this situation alive. There were too many close calls today."

His insides tightened at the sadness in her voice. "If I had my way, I'd take every single bullet for you. I'd rewind time so that I passed by the Fosters' place five minutes earlier instead of dawdling along the road. And then I'd go back even farther to when we were younger, and…" He stopped himself before he said something he'd regret.

Her brow furrowed. "And what?"

"And… I'd be there for you sooner."

She frowned and leaned away from him, hands pressed against his chest. "Is that really what you were going to say?"

How did she read him so well? "Would you believe me if I said yes?"

"Not at all."

He sighed. "I can't. It's a discussion that needs to wait until later, okay? It *can* wait. And what did you mean, 'it might be the wrong time for this'? Time for what?"

The corner of her mouth turned up in a half smile. "Time for what I suspect you're stopping yourself from saying, and for what I'm going to say without speaking."

Well, that made no sense. Maybe he needed to get her medical help even sooner. "Ellen—"

She placed one finger over his lips. "*Shh*. I'm trying to tell you something."

And then, silently, she removed her finger and pressed her mouth against his for an entire conversation without words.

Where she'd found the gumption to simply stop talking and kiss him, she had no idea. But she was both glad and relieved that she had. His arms tightened around her again, sliding up her back, but this time it had nothing to do with comforting her and everything to do with this moment of connection. Still, the distance between them seemed too great, and based on the way he responded in kind, she knew he felt the same way.

This was no sisterly peck on the forehead, no side-arm hug of friendship. These were years of unrequited affection combined with the rush of the past few days. Two hearts, united in mutual respect and attraction, had finally come together in a sweet moment that took her breath away—but in a welcome manner, nothing like the drowning sensation she'd felt earlier that night when reality had come crashing across her shoulders like a steel beam.

Finally, and all too soon, Leo pulled away. She saw joy and contentment and love reflected back at her, and she hoped he read the same thing on her face. But as he gazed into her eyes and they began to breathe easier, doubt slipped into his expression to replace the contentment. Worry gnawed at her insides.

"Ellen, you have no idea how long I've wanted to do that." His voice was soft, his words spoken with care. "But I promised your brother a long time ago that I wouldn't pursue you. He, uh…"

She knew where he was going with this—where *Jamie* had gone with it—and she didn't like it one bit. "He thinks I have too much of my mother in me. Thinks that being with someone in the RCMP, with the risk that they could lose their life at any time, is too great. That I'd be shattered if it ever happened." She kept her tone flat and matter-of-fact, trying not to betray the crushing disappointment that the joy of the moment had been stolen. When Leo looked away, she knew she'd spoken correctly. "We had this conversation not twenty minutes ago, didn't we? And you said yourself that Jamie was wrong. And if you made this promise a long time ago, that was before I am who I am today. I've grown up an awful lot since being eighteen years old. As have you. As has my brother."

Leo nodded but still seemed hesitant. She understood his reluctance, though she didn't have to like it. He respected her, but he respected his friend, too. And while she felt certain he'd agree that no one could tell her what to do with her life besides herself, she also recognized that Jamie's overbearing request came from a place of love and concern.

"Leo, if you don't want this, I'll understand. Just say the word. But if my brother is the one getting in the way…"

He leaned in and kissed her on the nose, melting the small wall she'd begun to build since he'd brought someone else into the room with them, so to speak.

"I do want this," he finally said. "And I

want to talk more about it in daylight, not alone in a motel bathroom after an exhausting day. I'd also appreciate the chance to speak to Jamie personally before we take this any further. Uh, whatever 'this' is."

"I can respect that. And I agree that it's probably the courteous move to let him know privately that there's something going on."

"Something that we'll talk about in the morning once we've rested up and cleared our heads a bit." His eyes widened as she frowned at him. "I don't mean cleared our heads about each other! I have a feeling that what just happened was a long time coming for both of us. I'm referring to clearing our heads about who could be orchestrating the thefts and why. If it's someone on the inside, there's got to be a solid reason why, and if the guy who got arrested or Hogan hasn't talked by the time the morning rolls around, we'll need to start strategizing how we're going to manage until the situation is resolved."

She couldn't help the smile that spread across her face. Even with everything that had happened, even with the trauma of her distant and recent past replaying over and over in her mind tonight, she at least had this one beautiful thing to cling to. Plus, they were safe for the time being. No one knew where they were, and she felt ready to get some rest, certain her body would finally allow her to sleep.

She heard a rumble outside, coming closer to the motel. It sounded like one of those big-rig trucks, probably a long-haul driver checking in for a few hours of shut-eye before his next eighteen-hour stint at the wheel.

"I agree," she said, returning his kiss on the nose. "Both about this being a long time coming and what we'll need to do tomorrow. Guess I'd better head back to my room and try to sleep again, in case—"

The rumbling drowned out her next words, and a fraction of a second later, the hotel room imploded.

FOURTEEN

Ellen screamed as the entire building shook. Leo dove to the floor, covering her with his body, but as quickly as it happened, the shaking stopped. She blinked as Leo sat up—and a second later, a chunk of ceiling collapsed into the tub, exposing the bathroom to the night sky. The walls around them remained standing, but her stomach churned with the anticipation of what she'd see when she looked out the bathroom door.

From where they sat on the floor, the motel room looked mostly intact. But when Ellen rose to her feet to stumble to the doorway, she gasped and nearly fell over again.

The cab of a semitruck sat hissing and rumbling inside the motel room. It had barreled directly into her room first, then Leo's room, and plunged halfway through the next before its momentum stalled from all the impacts—though the engine still appeared to be running.

Through the smoke and debris, she could make out several horrifying details. The motel bed was gone, either swept away or demolished by the truck, along with the side walls and most of the front wall.

She swallowed down a wave of sickness that crept up the back of her throat at a stark realization. Every pair of family-style rooms in the motel mirrored each other—so the rooms could share the pipes in the bathroom, saving money on plumbing for the motel—which meant that, based on the truck's trajectory, *her* bed had been the first thing destroyed when the truck smashed into the space where she was supposed to be sleeping.

Reality sank in.

"I was supposed to be in bed. Asleep. You would have been asleep in here." She whirled around. Leo's mouth hung open. He seemed just as shocked as she was—maybe more so. She'd never seen him at such a loss before. He looked utterly defeated. "Someone just tried to kill us by driving a semitruck into the motel. But no one is supposed to know we're here."

She inhaled deeply, a preemptive measure to stave off any panic or darkness that might encroach, but the dust of the demolished walls still filled the air and made her cough.

As she coughed, she thought she heard a new sound. A rustling, like soft steps from someone trying very hard not to be heard.

She froze and whispered, "What was that? Please tell me it's not what I think it is."

Leo bowed his head and closed his eyes for a moment before responding. "I thought I heard footsteps. I hope I'm wrong. But get ready."

"Ready? For what?" But he held his finger to his lips and tapped his ear.

The truck engine died. Someone was definitely shuffling around out there. Possibly several people.

"They're checking," he mouthed silently. "To make sure we're dead."

Terror sliced through Ellen's heart. She pointed at the hole in the ceiling. Could they climb up and escape across the remaining section of roof before someone found them? Leo followed her gaze, then nodded and pointed at the toilet and the sink. She understood. It was going to be tricky to climb up without being seen or heard, and they'd have to move quickly, but they had the advantage of being in the back of the motel unit and mostly sheltered by the walls of the bathroom.

God is *looking out for us*. The thought came swiftly and unexpectedly. But how else could she explain the fact that they'd both been sitting in the bathroom at the back of Leo's motel room, arguably the most sheltered and secure part of the two-room structure, instead of asleep in their beds? She had to assume that the outer wall of her motel room, which opened onto the side of the parking lot, had been destroyed—so if they'd been in *her* bathroom to have their conversation instead of Leo's, the people coming to check to make sure the truck had done its dirty work would have been able to look directly into the bathroom and see that they were still alive. Instead, they were facing away from any exterior wall, giving them a chance to escape.

She climbed onto the closed toilet lid, then onto the sink. Reaching up, she was able to curl her fingers around the edge of the sheared-off ceiling. The rough construction of the wall dug into her skin, but she concentrated on hoisting herself up and onto the flat section of roof that remained over the bathroom. Smoke rose from the truck's cab, obscuring the view toward the road. As Leo copied her movements and joined her on the roof, she thought she saw shadows moving around below.

"Now what?" she whispered. "Do we drop to the ground at the back of the building and make a run for it?"

Leo inched himself to the edge of the roof and looked down. "That's going to be our best play. We should try to get to the tree line and pick our way back to town—though I'm not entirely sure which direction that is. I'm not super familiar with where this motel is located. You?"

She shook her head. "I've never been here before, only driven past it a few times. I don't usually take this road when getting around."

He grimaced. "So we'll need to get to the main road first, figure out which direction we're heading, and then use the tree line for cover to get to— Get down!"

They flattened onto their stomachs as a light swung over them. Someone was shining a flashlight into the rooms and sweeping it around, checking for their bodies.

"We have to go *now*," Leo whispered.

Ellen couldn't have agreed more. She shimmied on her belly to the edge of the building, then pushed back so her legs and hips dangled over the side. As she slid farther to hang off the ledge, her arms burned with the effort of supporting her own body weight twice in one day. She pushed back and dropped. The impact onto the ground was not pleasant, but it could have been much worse. At least they didn't have to climb down the side of a building again.

Leo dropped beside her, hardly making a sound as he landed. Then he waved her forward. They dove into the tall grass at the back of the motel, crouching to make their way down the side of the building toward the driveway exit that would hopefully put them on the correct road back to town. Or even better, she hoped, they'd see a road sign from the edge of the motel property with the distances marked.

As they reached the edge of the road, she and Leo lay flat against the incline in the ditch, toes tucked to spring forward the instant they decided to move. Ellen risked a look back over her shoulder at the scene they'd left. The far half of the motel was in ruins, and it looked surreal to see a semitruck sitting inside a demolished building.

Where was the owner? She hoped they hadn't hurt him. If these thieves had been clever enough to figure out where she and Leo were and how to send a truck smashing into their beds, surely they'd have been smart enough to get the owner off-site, even if only for twenty minutes while the situation went down.

"How did they find us?" she whispered.

Leo's nostrils flared as he swept his gaze back and forth along the empty road. "I have an idea, but it doesn't make a whole lot of sense. The only way—"

One of the men rounded the corner of the motel. As he switched his lit flashlight from one hand to the other, the beam swept across the property. Before Ellen realized what was happening, the light illuminated her leg before continuing its trajectory. She clapped a hand over her mouth to stifle the gasp.

Maybe no one had noticed. Maybe they'd figured her leg for a log, or maybe she was too far away from the men for anyone to even be glancing her direction.

"Don't move," Leo said. "My vision at night isn't great, but I think they're looking over here. Light draws the eye. As soon as they turn back to the building, we have to move. It's definitely the same guys—bandannas and ball caps. Why can't they make this easier for us and not bother with their disguises in the dark?"

But footsteps started to approach. One of the men shouted to the guy with the flashlight. "Why isn't anyone checking around the perimeter? Weren't you supposed to be doing that? Go!"

And then the flashlight beam started to rise again, right toward them.

Ellen and Leo locked gazes, silently agreeing that it was indeed time to go. *Now.*

The beam hit Ellen's leg again. Simultaneously, they dug their toes into the side of the ditch and sprang over the top, hitting solid earth above.

They started to run, feet pounding the pavement on the dark, empty road.

But so did the thieves, and the thieves were the ones with long-range weapons.

Ellen's hopes plummeted.

Despite everything they'd survived so far, they weren't going to make it.

Leo's lungs strained as he and Ellen ran down the road in darkness. Seconds after they'd burst out of the ditch like runners at the starting block of a race, shouts and pounding feet had come up behind them—much faster than he could have anticipated. He tried to stay aware of Ellen's presence next to him, because if either of them stumbled, even a lost second could mean the difference between life and death.

The wet road had dried since the rainstorm

earlier in the day, but there was nothing easy about finding the strength to run after everything they'd already been through. Ellen's breathing had also grown heavy and strained, and the raspy wheeze of trying to catch her breath matched his own.

And then he heard it—the thing that sent the most fear into his heart.

The thieves had started firing at them.

Gunshots brought bullets whizzing through the air. Most seemed to go wide, kicking up dirt or bits of asphalt as the thieves attempted to target the two of them in the dark. He considered telling Ellen to weave, but he almost worried that they'd be doing the thieves a favor.

That was, until a buzzing zip grazed his ear. A centimeter to the right, and he'd have been dead.

Lord, what are we to do?

But before he'd finished his prayer, headlights illuminated the road ahead. Leo cringed at the bright light after so long in darkness, but he immediately pushed Ellen to the road's shoulder where the light wouldn't hit them directly—otherwise the headlights would provide the perfect backdrop, giving away their exact position and making them easier targets.

"Keep moving!" He dropped into the ditch

and led the way across the ground. "The light will draw their attention away from us being in here, but step carefully."

The car kept coming, but just when Leo thought the vehicle would speed past them and continue toward the armed thieves, the driver yanked the parking break to spin the car in a perfect semicircle. The passenger-side door flung open, and Leo stumbled to a halt to see Staff Sergeant Clyne inside. Then the red, yellow and blue stripe design on the side of the car came into focus.

"Hurry!" Clyne called. "They're right behind you!"

Leo scrambled up the bank and helped Ellen inside, but he chose to climb into the back, too, instead of taking the passenger seat up front. He didn't want to be out of reach in case the danger triggered another PTSD episode.

As soon as they were secure inside the car, Clyne took off down the road. He glanced in his rearview mirror several times, and Leo braced himself for the inevitable pings and thuds of bullets embedding in metal. But none came, so he risked a glance out the back window. He no longer saw men in the road, and it remained empty of vehicles.

"They saw the patrol car and scattered,"

Clyne growled. "Just like before. They won't get far, though. There's backup on the way."

"You called it in already?" Leo sat back in his seat as the staff sergeant nodded. "Thanks. You have impeccable timing, you know that?"

The staff sergeant chuckled, though Leo didn't find it funny. Curious, maybe. And a little disconcerting. "Sorry my intended delivery didn't reach you. There's a lot going on back at the station."

"We had creamer and sugar packets," Ellen mumbled. "What I don't understand is how they found us. I don't get it. Where can we go? Where is left *to* go?"

Leo took her hand, trying to offer a sense of grounding. "You're right. It doesn't make sense that they found us when only one other person knew where we were. Unless you mentioned it to someone?" He addressed the staff sergeant. "Or maybe there's a tracking device on your car."

In fact, the more he thought about the tracking device theory, the more it made sense. Both Jamie and Clyne had been working on this case since day one. Jamie had been the first to arrive on the scene at the Fosters', giving his partner or one of the other officers who'd come with him plenty of time and opportunity to add a tracker to his vehicle. And maybe to Leo's own car, too, since he and Ellen had easily been found at the Parks' home that first night. Or it could have happened on the second visit to the Fosters' house, when Jamie was on-site with the forensic crew. The staff sergeant had arrived at the scene shortly after they'd entered the house, leaving both cars exposed once again.

Clyne and Jamie had been champions for getting this case solved and the thieves caught, but even a theory about tracking devices on the cars didn't explain the one massive detail that didn't seem to fit: the community center. He and Ellen had ridden horses out to the community center, not exactly a trackable mode of transport. Though Jamie hadn't been the only one who knew they'd gone there—the briefing that had shared the info with other officers had happened before he or the staff sergeant expected an internal leak.

All of the pieces were getting harder and harder to link together, to justify how they interconnected with each other. Leo's RCMP training told him that he was missing something important, that he'd somehow willfully blinded himself to the obvious solution because he was too close to the case. But with adrenaline pumping through his veins and a constant sense of being on the run, he hadn't had a proper moment to sit down with a clear head and think all of the details through.

"Guess you two didn't manage to get any sleep, eh?" The staff sergeant watched them through the rearview mirror.

"No." Ellen sighed. "At this point I'm so beyond tired that I've hit that wall where I'm not sure I could actually fall asleep even if I tried."

"I hear you. Hey, you two mind if I roll down the windows for a bit? The air is still uncomfortably muggy after that rain and the sharp upswing in temperature afterward. Summer is definitely on its way." He lowered the window without waiting for a response. Leo glanced at Ellen, who shrugged but remained silent. There was puffiness around her eyes that he didn't recall seeing before, clear evidence of her level of exhaustion—but then again, he hadn't noticed much else earlier besides the way their lips had fit together so easily for the most perfect, precious kiss. It had been the culmination of something he'd been waiting for since the day he'd realized, at seventeen years old, that what he felt for Ellen was more than friendship.

And then a truck had smashed through the

motel and ruined their moment, chasing away their chance to understand what had just happened and what it meant for them and the future—and if it in fact meant anything at all, or if they had both simply been overcome with emotion in the moment.

He feared that possibility almost as much as he'd feared one of the thieves' bullets finding its mark.

"This might seem like an odd request, too," the staff sergeant continued, "but do you mind if I have a cigarette? It's been a long day and I'm feeling a bit overdone."

"Those things will kill you someday," Leo said, his standard reply, though he was a touch surprised to hear that the man indulged in that particular vice. Then again, he supposed it shouldn't come as too great a shock. Smoking was, unfortunately, a common habit among folks in the area. Every summer there were massive campaigns all over the province begging residents and visitors not to fling their spent but still burning cigarette butts into the grass or on the ground. More than one horrific forest fire had been started that way during the increasingly frequent dry seasons, and still the issue persisted.

"I know," Clyne said, pulling a lighter and a cigarette out of his pocket. He placed the cigarette between his teeth and used his free hand to light it. The stench of carbon and smoke hit the back of Leo's nostrils and he sneezed several times, his body trying to expel the foreign particles.

Ellen's hand suddenly clamped down on his forearm. He turned to her, still blinking after the sneezes. "I'm okay," he said. "I don't usually have such a sensitivity. Phew."

But her eyes remained wide and wild. She slid her gaze sideways toward Clyne and back to him, as though attempting to communicate something important.

"Everything all right back there?" Clyne asked, puffing his smoke out the window.

Leo frowned at Ellen. "I think so." *What?* he silently asked. She jutted her chin out, pointed to her nose and flicked her gaze sideways again. Leo gaped at her for a moment... until, all of a sudden, his mental fog began to lift.

But before his brain could uncover the whole picture, the staff sergeant yanked on the steering wheel, pulling the car sharply to the right and onto a narrow, darkened road. Or maybe a driveway. Leo couldn't actually see *where* they'd ended up, thanks to how tightly hemmed in they were by the forest on either side. Anxiety gnawed at him as he tried once again to find clarity in Ellen's silent gestures and how they related to everything they'd gone through.

"Good," said Clyne. He slammed on the brakes to stop the car, punched the gearshift into Park, unbuckled his seat belt and twisted around to face Leo and Ellen. "Then you won't see this coming, and I can be done with you both and get on with my life."

That was when Leo noticed the gun pointed directly at Ellen's heart.

FIFTEEN

"The cigarette, Leo." Ellen groaned. "He's smoking one of Hogan's cigarettes. He's the person Hogan gave smokes to, and he's the reason the man isn't talking. Old Hogan is probably scared out of his mind."

She watched as Leo's mouth opened and closed in shock. "I don't understand. Why are you doing this? You're an officer of the law. A *leader*. People look up to you, trust you. Have you been behind the thefts this entire time?"

Clyne's expression darkened. "You don't know me. You don't know my life or my situation, so I suggest you stop talking and accept your fate. You'll receive an honorable memorial befitting a fallen officer, Thrace. It's the least I can do, but trust me when I say I never expected any outsiders to get mixed up in this, least of all a fellow officer. You should have kept your nose out of it."

"And you should have realized that if I

wasn't sitting here, one of your own team members from the Fort St. Jacob detachment very well could be. If you're truly responsible for all of this, that means you're also responsible for the homicide of Rod Kroeker. As soon as that happened, you had to have known this was all going to unravel on you."

Clyne's hand holding the gun wobbled as the man grew angrier. Ellen hoped Leo had a plan, because she very well couldn't do anything from where she was seated—and she had a feeling that the more Leo kept the man talking, the more upset he'd get, and upset people tended to lose control of their trigger fingers. She squeezed Leo's forearm even tighter, hoping he'd get the message again, but his attention was wholly focused on the man with the weapon.

"All I needed to do was remove the eyewitness from the equation, and I could have ensured this entire interruption would blow over. Until you came snooping around."

"You think your whole town would have let Kroeker's death go unresolved? You think Jamie Biers would simply let his sister's traumatic eyewitness experience go? Not to mention, if you killed Ellen here, Biers wouldn't rest until he'd torn her killer limb from limb, metaphorically speaking. Though I wouldn't put anything else past him. And if you go through with killing her now, it'll still be a problem. You've lost your chance to take her out quietly."

Ellen stared at Leo. What was he saying? That the man should have killed her a long time ago? She had no idea where he was going with this—until she saw the uncertainty flash across the staff sergeant's face.

"I have no choice. This was all a victimless crime until *she* came along. My men got in, got out and no one got hurt. Those rich, spoiled folks in their ivory towers can afford to replace every single item. They have more money than they know what to do with, anyway. They won't feel the loss like some of us do when the government gets grabby with our income and refuses to give us what we deserve."

"But she didn't *come along*, Clyne. Your men made a mistake. You chose the wrong target, because she was already there. Your carefully orchestrated operation was doomed the moment you neglected to do due diligence and ensure your men were hitting the right house." Leo tilted his head and narrowed his eyes. "But your men weren't the only ones there, were they. You were there, too. This was *your* mistake."

Even in the darkness, Ellen didn't miss how the man's cheeks burned bright red, the creases in his forehead becoming even deeper the longer Leo kept him engaged.

"I said, stop talking. I have my reasons. You couldn't possibly understand."

"I understand that you're breaking the law. What I don't think *you* understand is how badly this is going to backfire on you once the two of us go missing. Between Ellen and me, we have three brothers and two parents who've served in the RCMP. No one is going to take this lightly. There's no possible way you can sweep our deaths under the rug and manage not to have them point back to you eventually. You even have a visiting forensics examiner in town. Do you honestly think she's not going to put all the pieces together?"

Clyne raised the barrel of his gun toward the car ceiling as though contemplating Leo's words. But all too soon, his face grew devoid of expression as he lowered it again—this time at Leo's forehead. "Trucco is a patsy. I have plans for her, too, if she interferes, and I've done my best to keep her off the scent so far…but as of tomorrow morning, she's on an airplane headed back to Ottawa and out of my hair for good. This is my territory, Thrace. I'll find a way. Trust me. I have no choice."

There it was. Ellen heard it in the man's voice, the depth of his desperation. There was something going on here that he wasn't telling them about, some critical factor that had driven him to break the law, forfeit his principles, risk his life and take the lives of others.

She spoke as softly and gently as she could, considering the circumstances. "There is always a choice, sir. No matter how bad you think it is. There's another way."

Sweat broke out along the man's forehead, and his throat bobbed as he swallowed hard. The gun trembled in his hand. "There isn't. That's been made abundantly clear. I can't lose... Never mind. It doesn't matter. Just know, if it makes you feel any better, that someone else's life will be saved through your sacrifice. Goodbye, Thrace."

A scream rose in Ellen's throat as the man's arm steadied, his finger beginning to squeeze the trigger. At the same instant, Leo dove sideways and kicked upward. His foot connected with the gun as it fired, sending the bullet through the roof. The gun toppled from Clyne's hand as the man cried out in surprise and pain. Leo rolled up and swung a fist into the staff sergeant's face.

The impact sent the man tilting toward the windshield, where his head bounced off the steering wheel. Clyne roared with fury and tried to return the punch, but since he had to twist to reach into the back seat, Leo still had the advantage. A second swing caught Clyne in the jaw.

"Get out, Ellen!" Leo shouted, but Ellen was already tugging on the door handle. It didn't budge.

"He's locked us inside."

"Of course he has," Leo growled. "I should have figured. This is a patrol car. Hang on and get ready to go as soon as I give the signal. Pull your feet up on the seat—we might have to go through the front."

She did as instructed, but Clyne had nearly shaken off the effects of Leo's fist connecting with his skull. The man made a grab for Leo, but since Leo had the position of advantage, he allowed Clyne to grab him and try to pull him forward. Ellen gasped as Leo used the leverage to propel himself into Clyne with force, slamming the staff sergeant's forehead into the center of the car's dashboard.

The impact made a horrible, cracking noise as pieces of police equipment collided with the man's face. As Clyne bounced off and flopped back into the seat, Ellen noticed a cracked screen and several buttons covered in blood. She thought she might be sick.

Leo pointed to the passenger door in the front. "He's out, but I don't know for how long. We need to move. Climb into the front seat and get out the passenger side. Go! I'll hold him off if he wakes up, go!"

Ellen couldn't move.

The thump. The sound of a skull on a hard surface.

Not again.

She couldn't catch her breath. Visions of her mother began to swim behind her eyes, images of Rod hitting the ground.

Strong hands gripped her shoulders and her vision refocused. Leo stared at her with—not pity. Not frustration. With confidence.

"You can do this. Ellen, I need you to do this. It's going to be hard, but if we don't get out of this car right now, we're going to die. You will never see Jamie again. My brother's wedding will be a funeral instead of a celebration. This is reality. We have to go, *now*."

You can do this. A voice inside told her she could. She didn't know where it came from or why, but a surge of energy welled up inside of her, and she knew they were going to make it out. God was looking out for them. Leo believed in her. She believed in herself.

She dove over the front seat and opened the passenger door, throwing herself out into the warm night air. Leo emerged right behind her, keys jingling in his hands.

"Should we get his phone?" she asked.

A low moan came from inside the car.

"No time," Leo said. "Grabbed his walkie and keys, but we've got to get out of here."

They faced the darkened road and ran.

By the time they reached the end of the road, they were both spent and out of breath. *Again.* Leo rested his hands on his hips and leaned over, trying to regather his strength. The road had long since curved and taken them out of view of the staff sergeant's patrol car, but Leo didn't want to take their temporary evasion for granted. The man could be on the move either on foot or in the car—though he hoped that taking the keys had delayed or eliminated the latter option.

Beside him, Ellen was studying the crossroad they'd emerged onto.

"Any ideas?"

She jogged a few meters in one direction, looked around, then doubled back. "We're heading back toward Schroeder Lake. I don't know what Clyne thought he'd do with our bodies after shooting us, but maybe he planned to dump us in the lake? Or in somebody's trash and hope we wouldn't be discovered until the residents returned? It makes no sense."

"I agree," he said, surprised at her casual discussion of their deaths. "But I think the man has reached a breaking point. From the sound of things, he's got a personal crisis happening and thinks that silencing us is the only way to solve his problem. If we had any idea what that problem is, maybe we'd have been better able to deal with him."

"Let's go this way." She waved him forward and they hurried down the road, though they both continued to breathe heavily from the exertion. "I don't want to run into a repeat of yesterday, but I'm not sure what else to do but find a phone and call for help."

He held up the walkie-talkie. "You don't think I should use this?"

She shrugged. "Is it even safe? How do we know that there's not someone else in the detachment who's working with him? Or what if Clyne has come to and is listening with the car radio somehow?"

"That's a good point." He sighed and shoved the device back into his pocket. "We need to get to a real phone and call your brother. Let him know what's happening."

"Agreed. And like I said, I don't want to repeat yesterday's incident, but..."

"You know how to get into the Schroeder Lake cottages, and our best option is calling from one of those landlines."

She pressed her lips together, almost apologetic. "Exactly."

"Clyne's not stupid. He'll anticipate that being our next move, so what we need to do is get there before he does or before he sends his people after us again. We'd better hustle."

Whether they'd make it to a cottage before their strength finally gave out was another matter entirely, so it was with an overwhelming sense of relief that they approached a green stake by the side of the road, the standard demarcation of the end of a driveway. But Ellen passed this one by, continuing onto the next. By the time they reached it, Leo was certain his legs would buckle under him, but they both found the strength to approach the house with caution.

The driveway was empty and the house dark. After checking several windows and seeing no shifting shadows inside, Leo decided that they needed to make a move rather than allow paranoia to prevent them from taking advantage of a possible lifeline.

Ellen entered the security code on the house and they slipped inside, closing the door behind them.

"Do we need to lock it with the code, too?" Leo asked as the door clicked into place. "Or does it auto-lock?"

"The system auto-locks it after two minutes," she said. "So unless someone breaks a window, we're good. I think there's a phone in the kitchen and one in the upstairs office."

"Let's go upstairs. There'll be less visibility from the outside."

Ellen led the way to the phone. Leo's legs burned at the effort of ascending the stairs to the second floor, and he was reminded that this cottage had been her second choice.

"Hey, why did we pass the first cottage? I'm not questioning your judgment, just curious. And exhausted."

"Because if Clyne anticipated our next move like you suspected he might, wouldn't he think we'd head to the nearest house?" She sighed and dropped into the desk chair, grabbing the phone receiver. "And I'd have gone farther if I thought we could both make it. I got worried that he'd be lying in wait outside the first house for sure and didn't want to risk it. Just in case."

"Wise move."

She dialed her brother and put the phone on speaker.

"Hello? Who's calling?" It sounded as though they'd woken him up.

"Jamie? It's me." Ellen's voice suddenly shook with emotion, her shoulders drooping at the sound of her brother's voice. Leo slipped around the back of the chair and placed his hands across her shoulders, gently kneading the knotted muscles there.

"Ellen? What's going on?" Jamie sounded instantly awake. "Where's Leo? Is he with you? Clyne said he had you in a secure place, but wouldn't tell me where—"

Leo leaned over the speaker. "I'm here with Ellen. Clyne is dirty. He's behind all of this. I don't know if there are other dirty cops in your detachment, but you need to grab some of the men you trust and get down to, uh—"

"The Dualas' place," said Ellen. "You know where that is? It's house number one-twenty-seven."

"Yes, I know where it is, but… Clyne? Are you sure?"

Leo laughed bitterly. "If you consider driving us down a dark road, pulling a gun and confessing to everything enough evidence to be sure, then yes. We're safe for now, holed up in this cottage, but there's no telling where Clyne is at the present. We left him knocked out in his patrol car, but he's not going to be too happy when he wakes up. And I don't want to risk running into him on the road."

"Okay." Jamie exhaled heavily. "Thank God you're all right. Hang tight. Don't go anywhere. I'll mobilize the cavalry and get there as fast as I can."

Ellen's finger hovered over the button to hang up, but another question sprang to mind and Leo jumped in, blurting it out before either Biers disconnected. "Hey, Jamie, do you know if the staff sergeant is having any personal issues? Family members or loved ones in trouble? Debt or legal problems that he's hinted at recently?"

Silence stretched on the other end of the line. When Jamie answered, he sounded uncertain. "I honestly don't know a lot about Clyne's personal life. He keeps work and home life extremely separate. Almost fanatically so. I did hear a rumor about a year and a half ago about his sister getting sick, though. Something about her husband taking off and leaving her with three kids to take care of while dealing with a life-threatening condition. I know Clyne had to unexpectedly take a week of his vacation time to visit her, and I got the impression that whatever she was going through, the Canadian health care system wasn't going to cover it. I

don't know specifics or if that's even an ongoing issue, though. Like I said, he doesn't
talk about his life outside of work, and what
I know is through hearsay."

"Thanks. See you soon." He ended the call.
Ellen looked at him quizzically. "That's it.
That *has* to be it. Why else would a man of
Clyne's position risk everything?"

She shook her head. "I don't know, though.
Why the thefts? We haven't had a chance to
learn much about what was stolen, and the
only information we do have is regarding a
valuable piece of artwork from a local auction."

"Which the staff sergeant may have very
well known about. If it was an auction of
high-value locally made goods, it stands to
reason that a police presence would have been
warranted. Community events can require a
police presence, depending on the size and
other factors. Working security at an auction
would give Clyne the perfect opportunity to
learn who purchased what, as well as the
value of all the items. The list of expensive
items to steal and resell would have been ba-
sically on display for him. And like he admitted, his team only stole items that wouldn't
matter to the residents in the long run. Local
artwork…who's going to claim that? Who's

going to make a stink about it? If someone can afford a twenty-thousand-dollar sculpture for their vacation home, it'd be hardly a drop in the bucket to buy a replacement, or even commission one from the original artist. No harm, no foul."

"Until someone died." Ellen pressed her hands against the sides of her head. "Why not back off? Why keep up the charade?"

Leo thought about it and shook his head in amazement. "Clyne kept up the charade, all right. Arresting one of his own men to throw us off the scent, allowing a visiting forensics expert to study the crime scenes. Showing up to rescue us and then grill us for information. Making sure to be in the right place at the right time to distance himself from the actual crew, after that incident with Rod on the first day. Ellen, if he has a sister in desperate health who can't work to pay her medical bills and who also has three children to feed, what other motivation does he need? RCMP salaries are good, especially at his level of leadership, but if she suffers from a rare or serious condition that isn't supported by health care, that can be a considerable amount of money out of pocket. Serious, crippling debt can become a reality."

Ellen stood and began pacing the room.

"It's all so extreme, though! Why go to such lengths? Why risk *so much*?"

"How far would Jamie go for you, Ellen?" Leo kept his voice soft. Ellen's gaze snapped to him in surprise. "Think about it. How far would Jamie go to keep you safe and healthy? What personal risks would he take? What personal risks would *you* take for him?"

Ellen's features fell, her indignant scowl sliding away as she sank back into the office chair. "I guess…there's never been a limit. And he's already done so much. He put his life on hold. He hasn't dated or taken any promotions, or even gone on a vacation in years. I can't remember the last time he did something for himself. He always jumps in to help and protect me, though I've never asked for it. I didn't realize…" She looked up again, a frown taking over her delicate features. "Clyne's love for his sister and his drive to protect her has become an obsession. I don't want that to happen with Jamie and me."

Leo sighed and took her hands. "It won't, but he may need to be reminded that you're not eighteen anymore, like you said earlier. That's a conversation you'll need to have with Jamie yourself. It's between the two of you. But anyone can see how much you mean to each other, and I suspect that if his sister is all Clyne has—and if she's in such desperate need—he's doing what he thinks he needs to in order to take care of her. It's heartbreaking…but I understand."

Ellen nodded and stood. "Me, too. Should we wait for Jamie downstairs? I don't want to waste another moment getting out of this mess—"

Beeping came from downstairs, followed by the click of the door unlocking. Leo looked at Ellen, whose eyes had grown wide. "Does Jamie know the code?"

She shook her head.

His stomach began to churn. "Have the Dualas come back to town early?"

She shook her head again.

"Then who…" He felt sick. He'd overlooked something very important. In their rush to figure out why, they'd forgotten to consider *how*.

The thefts hadn't been reported until weeks later, because there'd been no signs of break-ins. No evidence of forced entry.

But it made sense now. The thieves had been able to enter the homes undetected because the person leading the charge had the security codes for the houses. And who could obtain those codes via seemingly official methods, and find a way to eliminate the records of entry with a simple phone call or threat of legal action?

Clyne could. Clyne had the codes. Clyne knew how to get inside all the vacation cottages.

Including the place they were hiding in.

SIXTEEN

Ellen pressed her hands against her mouth to keep from screaming. The look of utter horror on Leo's face told her all she needed to know. *Clyne is in the house.*

She took in the room—desk, chair, filing cabinet, storage closet. Could they hide in the storage closet? It looked small, but their options were few. All they needed to do was stall until Jamie arrived with help. But he was all the way back in Fort St. Jacob and they were at Schroeder Lake, which meant it would take him at least fifteen minutes to reach the cottage.

She crept to the closet and placed her hand on the door. If she opened it and they climbed inside, Clyne might hear the door slide on its tracks. In the utter silence of the house, most sounds would be heard no matter from how far away.

Footsteps clacked against the hardwood

floor of the living room. The man wasn't even making an effort to hide his presence.

"I know you're here," he said. There was no mistaking it—the staff sergeant was beyond angry. He was livid and out for blood. If he found them this time, they wouldn't be escaping his clutches alive. "You might as well come out and get it over with. I promise to make this quick. Relatively so, anyway. Maybe a few surface wounds to make up for the ones you gave me."

His heavy steps crossed the room downstairs. It sounded like he'd stopped at the base of the stairs.

"If I were a cowardly officer and a slippery little mouse, where would I be?"

The stairs creaked. Ellen held her breath, certain that if she moved a single muscle, he'd hear it. At any minute, they'd be found.

Leo's fingers found the side of her face, and she gazed up into his eyes. She focused on the intensity there, giving her brain something else to do besides drag up sights and sounds from her memory.

And then the stairs creaked again, but farther away. He'd taken the split-level stairs from the living room to the kitchen instead of coming up to the second floor.

Leo leaned over to whisper directly in her

ear. "Is there a place to hide up here? Or an easy exit?"

"The back door is by the kitchen. There's a large closet in the master bedroom, like the Fosters' closet where you found me. But we'll have to hurry. If we don't want him to hear us opening the door and getting inside, we have to do it while he's at the back of the house."

Leo didn't hesitate. He tiptoed to the office door, paused to listen, then waved her over. She didn't hear Clyne downstairs, which she hoped meant he'd gone all the way to the back of the kitchen in search of them. If they'd been really quick, they might have been able to race out the front door, but there was no guarantee he wasn't lying in wait for them to do just that. It could be a trap.

She took careful, light steps from the office to the master bedroom, praying to a God who she thought just might be listening after all that the floor wouldn't creak under their weight.

They reached the master bedroom, and Ellen froze in front of the closet. The next few seconds would mean the difference between life and death. Would the closet slide open silently or rumble and squeak on its tracks? Had she used a spray lubricant on this closet the last time she was here, or not?

Leo's hand found her forearm, lending her strength.

She took a deep breath and slid open the door. It moved in silence and she exhaled in relief.

Then the stairs creaked again.

She dove inside the closet and Leo followed after her. He slid the door shut as the steps came closer, and although she hadn't been able to see in the dark exactly what was inside of this closet, she thought she felt a pile of terrycloth towels under her left hand.

Would Clyne remember her report about hiding in the Fosters' closet? Had he even read the report she'd given?

"Now who's being unreasonable?" said Clyne. It sounded as though he stood in the hallway outside the bedroom. "Delaying the inevitable isn't going to make it any better for either of us. We all know how this ends, so there's no point in expending so much effort. I'm going to find you, and the angrier I am, the more it'll hurt."

The steps came closer. To the doorway.

Ellen slid her shoulders against the back of the closet, sinking to the floor. There was no way out. He was going to find them, and there was nothing she or Leo could do anymore. This whole situation was going to end the same way it had started, with her crouching alone in terror inside a closet—no, not alone.

She had Leo. And he'd sunk down right next to her, placed his arms around her and drawn her close. She tucked into the crook of his shoulder, pressing her cheek into his sternum. He felt warm, solid and secure.

He felt like everything she'd ever wanted, just at the wrong time. In the wrong place.

"It's not personal," said Clyne. A shadow passed in front of the closet door. Ellen pressed her hands over her mouth again, trying with everything in her not to scream. Leo held her tighter, and she felt his breath grow even more silent and shallow. "But family comes first. And anyone who gets in the way of that, well…you know. One does what one must. I'm as sorry as anybody that Mr. Kroeker was in the wrong place at the wrong time, but these things happen. As they have to you. And once you're both out of the picture, I can get back to business—legitimate and otherwise." He chuckled at his own comment.

His fingers curled around the edge of the closet door. As the door slid back, Leo raised her face to meet her eyes.

"I love you, Ellen," he said.

A gun swung down toward them in the darkness.

SEVENTEEN

The front door slammed open with a bang as police sirens wailed through the air. A spotlight shone through the master bedroom window, illuminating Clyne as he stood with his weapon pointed inside the closet. He flinched and threw his hands in front of his face, momentarily blinded by the intense light.

Leo saw the opening, and he took it.

He burst out of the closet, knocking the gun upward. It discharged with a deafening crack, and he prayed he'd been fast enough that the bullet hadn't hit either himself or Ellen. Clyne, surprised and half blinded by the spotlight, was easily shoved off balance with the force of Leo's attack.

But Clyne didn't let go of the gun.

Leo stomped on Clyne's wrist. The gun fell from his grasp. The man roared in pain and leaped to his feet as Leo kicked the gun out of reach. Clyne wrapped his hands around Leo's throat and squeezed. His adrenaline-fueled grip made sparks fly in front of Leo's vision, and his lungs strained to take another breath.

"Police! Don't move!" Several voices shouted the command in near unison.

Thunderous footsteps came up the stairs. Leo's vision dimmed. The world became a series of bangs and loud shouts, and suddenly the pressure on his neck was gone. He fell to the ground, touching his throat and gasping for air, uncertain whether he'd ever be able to take another breath again.

Is this it, Lord? Is this how it ends for me? Please, take care of...

And then Ellen's face filled his whole world, and her lips found his, and he found himself unable to breathe for a completely different reason altogether.

When the room came back into focus, Ellen knelt on the floor in front of him. Clyne was nowhere to be seen, and various RCMP officers were rushing in and out of the room. A paramedic arrived to check for any immediate injuries and recommended that they both make their way to the ER once given the all clear, just in case. He found that it still hurt to breathe, but the paramedic didn't think his windpipe had been severely damaged, just bruised. Kind of like every other part of his body, and probably Ellen's, too.

After a long while that still seemed too brief, someone helped him and Ellen to their feet and escorted them outside the house. The early rays of morning light peeked above the treetops to the east. Had they really been on the run all night? The kiss, the truck smashing into the motel room...it all seemed so long ago.

"We're going to sit down for a second," Ellen told an officer, and she led Leo to the edge of the front porch. He sat next to her. "They took Clyne," she said. "You passed out for a few minutes, I think. I probably shouldn't have kissed you. The paramedic thought I'd done something, and I had to convince him that you'd been choked, not that I was such a great kisser I'd made you swoon."

"I'd laugh if it didn't hurt so much." He bumped her shoulder with his own. "But don't undersell yourself, Biers."

Her smile faded. "Biers? What's up with that? You always call me by my first name."

"Maybe passing out impacted me more than I thought it did." He glanced at her, but her jollity had diminished.

She lowered her voice. "Don't try to pull a fast one on me, Leo. I heard what you said in the closet, and I'm not going to forget it. Because I—"

"Ellen, we were in danger. I got emotional. I shouldn't have said it at all. It was a mistake." Her jaw dropped as her eyes filled with tears. It stung his heart to speak the words, but after what he'd just experienced, he knew it was the right thing to do. "I meant what I said. Please don't think I didn't. It was the wrong time to say it, is all. And I'm not convinced there will ever be a right time."

She shook her head. A tear rolled down her cheek. "I don't understand."

He inhaled deeply, searching for the right words. For what he could possibly say that would hurt her the least, while still conveying the depth of his affections for her. "We almost died multiple times over the past few days, but no moment came as close as it did in that closet. And it came even closer when Clyne wrapped his hands around my throat and squeezed. I was terrified, Ellen. I've never been that scared in my life, and do you know why?"

She shook her head, more tears flooding her beautiful face.

"Because I knew, in that moment, why Jamie asked me to stay away from you. Why he'd made me promise never to pursue you romantically. You've already lost enough people in your life, and I don't want you to have to worry about losing another—and as an RCMP officer, that danger is a reality every single day. Every time I go to work. Every time I take a call and head to a scene. Even a routine patrol can have unexpected consequences, which you've personally experienced in your family. Your brother is already an RCMP officer taking those risks, and while, God willing, nothing will ever happen to him, the possibility is there.

"There should be at least one person inside your heart who doesn't face death every day. The man you love, and who loves you, should have a safe, stress-free career. Something where you know that when he leaves in the morning, he'll come home at night. Where there's no chance of a stray bullet or a drunk citizen ruining everything. I don't want to see you hurt or in pain or scared of turning out like your mother, Ellen. I mean, I already know you're stronger than her. But I don't want to be the one to bring you another moment of heartache, and for that reason…"

"No." She shook her head a second time, each word shaky. "No, Leo. Don't do this. Please. I should be the one who gets to make that kind of choice. Not you."

"If I were to ever cause you an ounce of pain, Ellen, I couldn't live with myself."

Her sobs turned fierce and angry. She stood, towering over him. "But you're doing it right now. If you walk away from us, that's *exactly* what you'll be doing."

He shook his head and stood, too. Everything inside him screamed to take her in his arms again and tell her it would be all right. But that would be selfish. After everything he knew about her and her past, he couldn't be the one to make it worse. "If I walk away now, it will hurt for a few minutes. If I'm gunned down during an RCMP investigation, it will be so much worse. I do love you, Ellen. And that's why I'm letting you go."

He leaned forward to kiss her on the forehead one last time, but she leaned away, incredulous.

Everything hurt, but his heart hurt the most. He prayed that someday, she'd forgive him and find true happiness with the man God intended for her.

He prayed that someday, his own heart would heal.

Ellen watched in disbelief as he walked away. Shock ripped through every inch of her body, drowning out the physical pain and replacing it with a scream of utter fury and the deepest sorrow she could imagine.

It was all so much that she didn't know where to begin. Whether to run after him and beg him to reconsider, or whether to strike his name from her memory forever.

Because the truth was, she loved him, too, and he'd refused to give her a chance to say it.

She sank back down onto the porch steps, her vision growing hazy as her emotions took over and forced out every remaining drop of liquid through her tear ducts.

"Hey, sis." Jamie's voice brought her back to reality. He sat next to her and wrapped his arm around her shoulder. "I, uh… Look, I probably shouldn't have been listening just now. And there are a ton of other things that I need to be doing, and that *you* need to be doing, including getting to the ER to be checked over and giving your official testimony on what happened tonight. But did I just overhear Leo say that he loves you?"

She nodded, but couldn't bring herself to speak.

"Hmm. And I take it that wasn't in an 'oh, I love you because we've been friends for years and we survived this ordeal together' type of way?" When she didn't respond, he sighed heavily and buried his head in his hands. "I thought so. This is all my fault."

"What?" She found her voice, and she couldn't believe Jamie's words. "All *your* fault? Why, because you asked him to stay away from me years and years ago?"

"Well, yeah." Jamie shrugged, looking sheepish. "I didn't even realize you knew."

"I figured it out a long time ago. It's not news to me, and Leo more or less admitted as much."

"And you're not furious with me?"

She rolled her eyes. "You're my brother. You've always been overprotective—it's what brothers do. But you're also not heartless. You know I'm my own person and can make my own decisions."

"You always have." He smiled with one side of his mouth, but it wasn't a happy expression. "So, uh… I saw the way Leo looked at you just now. And how he's been looking at you for a while. I mean, to quote a certain sister, I figured it out a long time ago. About what he feels for you, I mean."

She had no idea why Jamie was even talking to her about this. "So? It doesn't matter anymore. He claims he loves me, but he doesn't want anything to do with me. I guess it was all heat of the moment, emotion-driven stuff."

Jamie sighed again and gently kicked at her foot. "Or Leo is an honorable man, doing what he thinks is right based on all the 'Ellen is fragile and if you hurt her I'll end you' garbage that I poured into his skull for years and years. I was trying to look out for you, and honestly, if we went back in time, I'd do it again. But we're both adults now. You're more than capable of taking care of yourself, and Leo is clearly—based on what just happened—the type of person to put others' needs before his own. If he's willing to make a massive sacrifice like walking away from you despite being madly in love with you, just so he doesn't cause you harm, then he's exactly the kind of man you deserve. I mean, I think he's good enough for you, and that's a hard position to be in, in my eyes. I shouldn't have…"

Jamie growled and tilted his head to the sky. "You know what I did? I forced my best friend to choose between friendship and love for far too long, and it was wrong. I need to speak to him and make it right. And then I'm going to smack him upside the head and tell him to make things right with you. Okay?"

Ellen wasn't sure it actually *was* okay, but she nodded, anyway. Jamie gave her a quick side-hug and hurried away, heading in the direction Leo had wandered.

She hoped that Jamie's words would be enough to convince Leo of the truth—that loving her was exactly what she wanted. That Jamie had been wrong, which Leo had even admitted. She hoped that hearing that confession from Jamie himself would change Leo's mind, because she certainly didn't know how to change his mind.

I need to tell him I love him.

He hadn't given her the opportunity to say it, and she ached to speak the words aloud. Maybe it would help him see that by walking away, he was hurting her more than any risk-laden career ever could—that his choice to leave for the sake of a situation that might not even happen was, in fact, the most selfish thing he could do.

She stood and waited for Jamie to return with Leo, but when several minutes turned into many, she began to wonder if either of them was coming back.

Just when she'd started walking toward a waiting patrol car that had arrived to take her back to the station, Jamie came running down the driveway.

"Hey! Is Leo with you?" he shouted as he ran.

Alarm constricted her insides. "No," she called back. "Why?"

"Oh, no. I'm so sorry." Jamie skidded to a halt, his features fallen in dismay and sadness.

She didn't understand. "What are you taking about?"

Jamie's limbs drooped with defeat. "Ellen… he's gone."

EIGHTEEN

Three weeks passed without a word from Leo. He wasn't answering his phone calls or emails, and his brothers clammed up when she tried to get in touch with them. After the first few days, Jamie admitted that he'd spoken to Leo on official police business—of course they'd needed Leo's full testimony against Clyne and his crew, whose motivation for organizing and committing the numerous thefts had indeed been to financially support his critically ill sister, as Leo and Jamie had suspected—but that Ellen might want to be patient.

Ellen appreciated the heads-up, but she had an awful, sinking feeling that Jamie's words meant that he'd tried to talk some sense into his friend and Leo hadn't seen reason.

The last thing Ellen wanted to do was grovel. She had her pride, and begging was out of the question. But what Leo had done wasn't fair or respectful to either of them—he'd said his piece and walked away without giving her the chance to say hers. And she was going to make sure she was heard, even if it meant it was the last time they ever spoke to each other.

She hoped it wouldn't be. But her heart feared the worst.

Still, she woke up the morning of Sam and Kara's wedding, dressed in her favorite tawny skirt and forest green sweater, tamed her hair as much as could be reasonably expected for a public appearance, and marched down to the church where the wedding was to be held at one o'clock that day. While she had to swallow down a touch of guilt for intending to intercept Leo on his brother's wedding day, she figured that he had it coming by not speaking to her before the day arrived.

And he definitely wouldn't be able to avoid her by skipping the wedding.

She arrived an hour early, fully intending to plant herself inside the doorway so she wouldn't miss Leo's arrival and he wouldn't see her until it was too late—and too awkward—to turn around and bolt back down the church steps.

But when she flung open the door, slipped inside and scanned the flower-draped foyer for a good place to lie in wait, she saw him. Her stomach tightened with sudden, inexplicable, nervous fear.

Leo sat on a bench at the far end of the foyer, head buried in his hands.

The heavy church door thudded into place behind her and she jumped, startled. At the sound, Leo looked up sharply—and saw her.

She couldn't breathe.

"Ellen." His voice was low and soothing, the way she remembered it being in every instance of danger, in every moment of stillness.

She barely managed more than a whisper. "Hi."

He dropped his head again, placed his hands on his knees and stood. Her back bumped against the door as he approached her.

"I thought I might find you here," he said. A tiny, hopeful smile curved the corner of his mouth, but she blinked in surprise.

"Wait, what? You thought *you'd* find *me* here?" She looked around the empty foyer. "I came here to wait for *you*. But shouldn't you be with your brothers right now?"

"Nah. Everyone's finishing getting dressed and will head over in a bit. I just rushed the process, because…"

She held up her hand, unfreezing her body and pushing through the nerves. "No. You don't get to talk yet." He frowned in confusion. "Leo, you said a whole lot of things a few weeks ago, and then you walked away. You didn't let me give my side. And for someone who claims to love me, that was a terrible, disrespectful way to show it."

His face fell, but he nodded. "I know. That's why I'm here, to apologize."

"Then I accept your apology. You don't need to say anything else, because I think you've said quite enough." He opened his mouth as if to speak again, but she held up one finger and he pressed his lips together instead. "Leo, you said yourself that what you and Jamie talked about was maybe necessary back when we were teenagers. I *was* fragile. I *was* in a delicate state. I should have sought medical help, but we had almost no support and no family members up here to help us navigate those waters after my mother died. Jamie tried to be my father and my mother and my brother, and I needed that for a time. But we're adults now. He sees that as well as I do. It's time for him to move on and live his own life instead of clinging to mine. We needed that codependency to keep each other afloat after our parents' deaths, but we're our own people now, with our own lives. Our own careers. Our own capacity for love outside of the safety of each other. And, Leo, I do love you. I think I always did, in a way, but these past few weeks showed me what's been missing in my life, and it's you. You understand my past and you accept my present. You care about my future, and you're patient with me where my faith—and doubts—are concerned. No one else has ever come close. No one else has truly seen and accepted me, issues and all, before you. I love you and I want to be with you, but not if you're going to contradict the very things you said to me when we were on the run. Not if you're going to let the needs of the past cloud the possibility of the future. This is between me and you. No one else."

Ellen's throat constricted as soon as she finished speaking. Her pulse raced and she felt light-headed as they stood in silence. Was this where it all ended for them? Before their time together had even truly begun?

And then, unexpectedly, Leo's eyes welled up with tears. He didn't even try to stop them as they poured forth, and she let it happen— just as he'd allowed her the emotional release she'd needed when they'd sat in the little motel room on the highway.

When he finally caught his breath, he

heaved a sigh laden with meaning. "Ellen, you're right. About everything. I shouldn't have let irrational fear cloud my judgment, and it was wrong of me to walk away. And then after I'd thought about it and realized what I'd done, I was sure you'd never forgive me. I racked my brain for weeks on how to make it up to you, and it took me far too long to realize what I should have done the moment I knew I was in the wrong. I should have immediately apologized and begged your forgiveness, and let you know that I *do* know who you are today isn't who you were in the past.

"During our time together, you showed me what it means to be strong. You struggle with a serious mental health issue, and yet you still face obstacles head-on. You're loyal to family and friends, and you're clever and inventive in moments of crisis. Not having you around these past few weeks has been one of the hardest times of my life. It might sound unbelievable, but over the course of what we went through, you became my rock. My touchstone. I believe God brought us back together for a reason, to show me that I'd been too focused on myself and on pleasing others. I tried not to rock the boat. Well, my boat got rocked the moment you attacked me with that bottle of bleach, and I'd happily let it happen again if it meant we could take our past and our present and meld it into a beautiful future. But I know that might not be possible. And whatever you want, I'll respect. I won't try to decide for you ever again."

A strange sensation welled up inside her chest. *Is this...is this what joy feels like, God?*

She hadn't felt like this in a very, very long time. The sincerity in his voice and the love reflected in his expression were exactly what she had hoped for and what she hadn't known she needed.

He loved her. She loved him. And it was as simple as that.

"What kind of a future, Leo?" She couldn't help smiling, and she hoped he heard the teasing in her words.

But then he shrugged and winked. "Well, I know what I'd be in it for. And while some might say it's too fast, I'd say to them that we've known each other for a very long time, and I've never wanted to spend my life with anyone as much as I want to spend it with you." He lowered himself to one knee. "So, this is the future I want—one with you permanently in it. Ellen Biers, will you marry me?"

She gasped. "Leo...are you serious?"

He frowned. "That's not exactly the answer a man hopes to hear when he's down on one knee."

He *was* serious. And why shouldn't he be? They were perfect for each other, and she knew with every part of her heart that this was exactly the kind of future she wanted, too.

"Yes," she said, laughing. "Yes, I will marry you. How's that for an answer?"

"Well, I wasn't going to make up your mind for you," he said, standing. "And I know I said I'll never do it again. But I kind of have a feeling that you want to kiss me now as much as I want to kiss you."

"And this time," she said, heart soaring with gratitude and love, "you've got it right."

* * * * *

If you enjoyed this story,
look for the first book in the
Mountie Brotherhood series,
Wilderness Pursuit.

Dear Reader,

Thank you for spending your reading time with Leo and Ellen! I enjoyed writing the middle Thrace brother's story, and I hope you enjoyed the cameo appearances of Sam and Kara from *Wilderness Pursuit*. That's two brothers matched up and one to go!

While Ellen was able to begin to accept her struggle with PTSD in this story, the reality is that PTSD is a complex and serious issue that affects many individuals, for myriad reasons. It should only be diagnosed by a medical professional, so if you or someone you know is struggling, please seek professional assistance. You may also find comfort in organizations such as the National Center for PTSD (USA: www.ptsd.va.gov) or the PTSD Association of Canada (www.ptsdassociation.com).

Please remember that God loves you and wants the best for you—and so do I! We live in a broken world where terrible things happen, but He has given us free will to make our own choices, for better or worse, because He loves us so much. It can be hard to see the reason for these struggles, and they won't always make sense in our time. Know that

God is there with you, on the good days and the bad, and He will never, ever abandon His children.

I love hearing from readers. Connect with me at michellekarl.com or find me on Twitter @_MichelleKarl_. Thank you so much for reading *Accidental Eyewitness*!

Blessings,
Michelle

Get 4 FREE REWARDS!

We'll send you 2 FREE Books
plus 2 FREE Mystery Gifts.

Love Inspired® books feature contemporary inspirational romances with Christian characters facing the challenges of life and love.

FREE
Value Over
$20

YES! Please send me 2 FREE Love Inspired® Romance novels and my 2 FREE mystery gifts (gifts are worth about $10 retail). After receiving them, if I don't wish to receive any more books, I can return the shipping statement marked "cancel." If I don't cancel, I will receive 6 brand-new novels every month and be billed just $5.24 for the regular-print edition or $5.74 each for the larger-print edition in the U.S., or $5.74 each for the regular-print edition or $6.24 each for the larger-print edition in Canada. That's a savings of at least 13% off the cover price. It's quite a bargain! Shipping and handling is just 50¢ per book in the U.S. and 75¢ per book in Canada*. I understand that accepting the 2 free books and gifts places me under no obligation to buy anything. I can always return a shipment and cancel at any time. The free books and gifts are mine to keep no matter what I decide.

Choose one: ☐ **Love Inspired® Romance**
Regular-Print
(105/305 IDN GMY4)

☐ **Love Inspired® Romance**
Larger-Print
(122/322 IDN GMY4)

Name (please print)

Address   Apt. #

City   State/Province   Zip/Postal Code

Mail to the **Reader Service:**
IN U.S.A.: P.O. Box 1341, Buffalo, NY 14240-8531
IN CANADA: P.O. Box 603, Fort Erie, Ontario L2A 5X3

Want to try two free books from another series? Call 1-800-873-8635 or visit www.ReaderService.com.

*Terms and prices subject to change without notice. Prices do not include applicable taxes. Sales tax applicable in N.Y. Canadian residents will be charged applicable taxes. Offer not valid in Quebec. This offer is limited to one order per household. Books received may not be as shown. Not valid for current subscribers to Love Inspired Romance books. All orders subject to approval. Credit or debit balances in a customer's account(s) may be offset by any other outstanding balance owed by or to the customer. Please allow 4 to 6 weeks for delivery. Offer available while quantities last.

Your Privacy—The Reader Service is committed to protecting your privacy. Our Privacy Policy is available online at www.ReaderService.com or upon request from the Reader Service. We make a portion of our mailing list available to reputable third parties that offer products we believe may interest you. If you prefer that we not exchange your name with third parties, or if you wish to clarify or modify your communication preferences, please visit us at www.ReaderService.com/consumerschoice or write to us at Reader Service Preference Service, P.O. Box 9062, Buffalo, NY 14240-9062. Include your complete name and address.

LI18

Get 4 FREE REWARDS!

We'll send you 2 FREE Books
<u>plus</u> 2 FREE Mystery Gifts.

Harlequin® Heartwarming™ Larger-Print books feature traditional values of home, family, community and most of all—love.

FREE
Value Over
$20

YES! Please send me 2 FREE Harlequin® Heartwarming™ Larger-Print novels and my 2 FREE mystery gifts (gifts worth about $10 retail). After receiving them, if I don't wish to receive any more books, I can return the shipping statement marked "cancel." If I don't cancel, I will receive 4 brand-new larger-print novels every month and be billed just $5.49 per book in the U.S. or $6.24 per book in Canada. That's a savings of at least 19% off the cover price. It's quite a bargain! Shipping and handling is just 50¢ per book in the U.S. and 75¢ per book in Canada*. I understand that accepting the 2 free books and gifts places me under no obligation to buy anything. I can always return a shipment and cancel at any time. The free books and gifts are mine to keep no matter what I decide.

161/361 IDN GMY3

Name (please print)

Address   Apt. #

City   State/Province   Zip/Postal Code

Mail to the **Reader Service:**
IN U.S.A.: P.O. Box 1341, Buffalo, NY 14240-8531
IN CANADA: P.O. Box 603, Fort Erie, Ontario L2A 5X3

Want to try two free books from another series? Call 1-800-873-8635 or visit www.ReaderService.com.

HOME on the RANCH

YES! Please send me the **Home on the Ranch Collection** in Larger Print. This collection begins with 3 FREE books and 2 FREE gifts in the first shipment. Along with my 3 free books, I'll also get the next 4 books from the Home on the Ranch Collection, in LARGER PRINT, which I may either return and owe nothing, or keep for the low price of $5.24 U.S./ $5.89 CDN each plus $2.99 for shipping and handling per shipment*. If I decide to continue, about once a month for 8 months I will get 6 or 7 more books, but will only need to pay for 4. That means 2 or 3 books in every shipment will be FREE! If I decide to keep the entire collection, I'll have paid for only 32 books because 19 books are FREE! I understand that accepting the 3 free books and gifts places me under no obligation to buy anything. I can always return a shipment and cancel at any time. My free books and gifts are mine to keep no matter what I decide.

268 HCN 3760 468 HCN 3760

Name	(PLEASE PRINT)	
Address		Apt. #
City	State/Prov.	Zip/Postal Code

Signature (if under 18, a parent or guardian must sign)

Mail to the **Reader Service:**

IN U.S.A.: P.O. Box 1341, Buffalo, New York 14240-8531
IN CANADA: P.O. Box 603, Fort Erie, Ontario L2A 5X3

READERSERVICE.COM

Manage your account online!

- Review your order history
- Manage your payments
- Update your address

We've designed the
Reader Service website
just for you.

Enjoy all the features!

- Discover new series available to you, and read excerpts from any series.
- Respond to mailings and special monthly offers.
- Browse the Bonus Bucks catalog and online-only exculsives.
- Share your feedback.

Visit us at:
ReaderService.com